DEAD MAN'S HAND

A MAFIA ROMANCE

RENEE ROSE

Copyright © October 2019 Dead Man's Hand by Renee Rose

Published in the United States of America

Renee Rose Romance

Editor: Maggie Ryan

This book is a work of fiction. While reference might be made to actual historical events or existing locations, the names, characters, places and incidents are either the product of the author's imaginations or are used fictitiously, and any resemblance to actual persons, living or dead, business establishments, events, or locales is entirely coincidental.

This book contains descriptions of many BDSM and sexual practices, but this is a work of fiction and, as such, should not be used in any way as a guide. The author and publisher will not be responsible for any loss, harm, injury, or death resulting from use of the information contained within. In other words, don't try this at home, folks!

ACKNOWLEDGMENTS

Thank you to Rhonda Butterbaugh for coming up with the title for this book. *Dead Man's Hand* fit Gio perfectly and the Man Who Lived (yep, I'm a Potterhead. Who isn't?). Thank you to Maggie Ryan for her edits and to Aubrey Cara, Tess Summers and Misty Malloy for beta reads!

All my love to the Romper Roomies. If you're not a member of my Facebook group, please send me an email at reneeroseauthor@gmail.com to join!

WANT FREE RENEE ROSE BOOKS?

Click here to sign up for Renee Rose's newsletter and receive a free copy of *Theirs to Protect, Owned by the Marine*, *Theirs to Punish, The Alpha's Punishment, Disobedience at the Dressmaker's* and *Her Billionaire Boss*. In addition to the free stories, you will also get special pricing, exclusive previews and news of new releases.

PLAYLIST

Piano Playlist

Solfeggietto by C.P.E. Bach
   Get Lucky by Daft Punk
   Birthday by The Beatles
   The Scientist by Coldplay
   Always a Woman by Billy Joel
   Piano Man by Billy Joel
   Hallelujah by Leonard Cohen
   Paint it Black by the Rolling Stones
   Marry Me by Train
   Marry You by Bruno Mars
   Marry Me by Dean Martin

CHAPTER 1

 io

FIRST THE BURNING. Then the blood seeping through my fingers. Always the sound of Paolo croaking my name over the crack of more gunfire.

Gio, no!

Gio's hit!

It's the horror of loss ringing in his voice that makes my heart pound. Not the pain. Not my own fear of death. I don't think about my demise in the moment. I didn't when it actually went down, and I don't in the nightmares that plague me every night.

And always the girl.

She's in every nightly replay. Sometimes she gets shot, too. Those are the worst. My inability to rescue her, to protect her from damage makes me want to die right there.

Other times she runs to me, after I've been shot. She wraps her arms around me and we both fall down.

Always her wide blue-green eyes lock onto mine the moment the first gun fires. I watch the terror fill them as the bullet tears through my middle.

That's the moment that keeps her in my dreams. In that split second, in the window where I'm sure I'm going to die, hers is the face I see. My fears are for her safety, and my anguish over being shot is that I can't protect her.

In her gaze, I swear I see it all mirrored back at me. She, too, thinks I'm going to die, and her anguish is in not warning me in time.

Because she tried. I remember every millisecond of that part. The five breaths before I got shot. I remember the way she tried to signal with her eyes. The way she refused to leave and get to safety, even though she had to know her cafe was about to explode in glass and wood and bullets and blood.

She's like an angel in the dreams—her pale face the beacon I use to understand my own death.

Only I don't die.

I didn't die.

And you'd think that would make everything crystal clear. The whole near-death experience thing. It's supposed to make you realize what you regret. What you desire. And then you get a second chance to make good on life.

Instead, I'm trapped in a nightmare-induced fog. Trying to untangle the meaning while I go through the motions of living.

The Caffè Milano girl doesn't have the answers—I don't know why or how my subconscious assigned so much meaning to her. She was just caught in the middle of a bad scene between the Russian *bratva* and our outfit.

And yet I can't get her out of my mind.

The angel of my death.

Near-death.

Marissa. An innocent girl I have no business sullying.

A girl who already saw too much.

A liability.

Marissa

SOME THINGS you can't forget. You can't unsee. Can't unhear.

Blood all over these floors. The sound of gunshots. The way my heart stopped when Junior Tacone pointed that gun at me, deciding whether to let me live or die.

I hate this time of day when the customers thin out, business gets slow, and I only have time to remember.

It's been six months since the battle between the Russian and Sicilian mafia went down in Caffè Milano, and I'm still jumpy as hell. Still examining every customer who comes in, praying he's not Russian mafia come for revenge. Or to shake me down for information on how to find the Tacones.

But they haven't come. No one ever came except the Tacones with their window repair guys and a large enough amount of money to upgrade our whole kitchen. Which was good because our walk-in cooler was inches away

3

from dying and this place hasn't had a remodel since my grandparents opened it in the 1960s.

I pull a bowl of pasta salad from the deli case to put in the walk-in overnight. When I come back, I freeze, a gasp hitting the back of my throat.

At first, I think it's Junior Tacone standing at my deli counter.

The guy who went gangster on my place and gunned down six guys. The one who is supposedly the protector of this neighborhood.

It's not Junior, though. It's his brother, Gio Tacone, the one who took a bullet out on the sidewalk. The man I thought was dead.

"Mr. Tacone!" I curse myself for sounding breathless.

"Gio," he corrects. "Marissa, how are you?"

He knows my name!

That's more than I can say for Junior, the current head of the family. And I wish it didn't do fluttery things to my insides, but it does. Gio rests a forearm on the counter and pins me with a dark-lashed hazel gaze.

He is pure man-candy. With those chiseled good looks, he could easily have been an actor or model, and he has the charm to match.

"You're alive," I blurt. I hadn't heard that he survived. I checked the newspapers and Googled his name after the shooting, and there weren't any reports of his death, but I saw him take a bullet with my own eyes. "I mean, you made it. I'm so glad." Then I blush, because, yeah. I'm probably not supposed to talk about what happened, even though it's just the two of us here.

Gio catches my wrist, stilling my hand. His thumb

4

strokes over my pulse as my fingers tremble in the space between us. "Why are you shaking, doll? You scared of me?"

Scared of him? Yes. Definitely. But also excited. He's the one Tacone brother I look forward to seeing. Always have, even when I was just ten years old, wiping tables down while the mafia men met.

"No!" I pull my hand away. "I'm just jumpy. You know—since… what happened. And you startled me."

His gaze penetrates, like he knows there's more to it than that, and he wants to know it all. A curious shifting happens in my chest.

I tuck an errant strand of hair behind my ear to cover my mounting discomfort.

"You have nightmares?" he guesses, like he's read my mind.

I give a single nod. Then it occurs to me how he knows. "Do you?"

I don't expect him to confess it if he does. I come from an Italian family. I know the men don't admit weakness.

So, I'm surprised when he says, "All the fucking time." He touches the place where the bullet must've gone in.

"Wow."

The corners of his lips quirk into a devastating grin. The man really should have gone into show business. "What? You think real men don't have nightmares?"

"Maybe not the men in your line of work."

The smile fades and he arches a brow. Oops. I crossed some line. I guess you don't mention a mobster's line of work.

5

I ignore the increased thumping of my heart. "Sorry. Is that something we don't talk about?"

He makes me sweat for two beats then gives a half-shrug, like he decided to let it go. "I didn't come here to ride your ass; I came to check on you. Make sure you're okay." He blinks those dark curly lashes that would be feminine except for the manly square jaw and aquiline nose. "Sounds like you're having a hard time."

The danger bell starts tolling in my head.

Never accept a favor from the Tacones. You'll pay for it for the rest of your life.

That's what my grandfather used to always lament. He borrowed from Arturo Tacone to start his business, and it took him forty years to pay off. But pay it off he did, and he was damn proud of it, too.

"I'm fine. We're fine." I straighten and lift my chin. "But we'd appreciate it if you'd hold your business meetings somewhere else in the future." I don't know what makes me say it. You don't piss off a mob boss by insulting him or making demands. I definitely could've found a nicer way to make my request.

Again, he considers me for a moment before answering. My palms get clammy but I keep my head high and meet his gaze.

"Agreed," he concedes. "We didn't expect trouble. Junior regretted what happened to this place."

"Junior pointed a gun at my head." The words tumble out and crash between us. Too late to take them back.

"Junior would never hurt you." He says it so immediately I know he believes it's true. But he didn't see what I saw. That moment of hesitation. The murmuring of his man beside him that I'm a witness.

He thought about killing me.

And then decided not to.

Gio catches my hand again and holds it, stroking the back of it this time. His fingers are large and powerful, making mine appear small and delicate in comparison. "That's why you're jumpy, huh? I'm sorry you got scared, but I promise you, you're safe. This place is under our protection."

I swallow, trying to ignore how pleasant his touch is. How nice it is to be soothed by this beautiful, dangerous man. I summon more bluster. "Maybe it would be better if it wasn't." My voice doesn't come out steady. There's a wobble to it that betrays my nerves. I clear my throat. "You know, if you just left us alone."

I hold my breath, tensing for his reaction.

Huh.

If I didn't know better, I would say my words hurt Gio rather than pissed him off. But he just shrugs. "Sorry, doll. You can't get rid of us. And you're on my watch now. Which means you're perfectly safe."

I want to tell him I'm not his doll and he can take his protection and fuck off, but I'm not insane. Also, some traitorous part of me wants him to keep stroking my hand, keep studying me like I'm the most interesting person he's seen all day.

But I know all that's a lie.

Gio's a player. And my body's response to his presence is dangerous.

Gio abandons my hand in favor of cupping my chin.

RENEE ROSE

"You're mad. I get it. I'll let you show me a little claw today. But we paid restitution to your family and will honor our commitments to this neighborhood and to Caffè Milano."

His touch is commanding and firm, but still gentle. It makes the flutters in my belly grow more wild.

"Gio," I murmur, turning my face away from him and out of his hand. My nipples are hard, rubbing against the inside of my bra.

He pulls a hundred dollar bill out of his pocket and drops in on the counter. "Give me two of those cannoli." He points to the case.

I obey wordlessly and tuck the hundred in my apron pocket, not bothering to offer him change. I figure if he used a hundred, it was because he wanted to throw his money around, and I'm going to let him do it.

He smirks a little as he takes the plate with the cannoli and sits down at a table in the cafe to eat them.

Fuck. I am so screwed.

Gio Tacone just decided to make me his pet project. Which means the chances of him ending up owning me just shot sky high.

Gio

I CAN'T BELIEVE I just told the Milano girl I have nightmares.

It's not something I've said aloud before. Who the fuck

would I tell, anyway? Junior would tell me to man up and get over it. Paolo would probably punch me where the bullet went in and then say, "See? You're fine."

And my ma? She doesn't even know I got shot. We keep the women out of our shit show.

But no, I haven't been the same since. And it's not that I didn't heal—although even that was touch and go for a while there. But I can't stop thinking about dying now.

Everywhere I look, I see people who could die today without being prepared. A guy crosses the street without looking and boom! He gets hit by a cab. Or some poor sot has an aneurism and croaks while out getting the mail.

No chance to say goodbye. To wrap up loose ends.

That could've been me.

And everywhere I go, I also see potential shooters. I'm looking over my shoulder for the *bratva* assholes, even though I know the saga's over. They kidnapped my sister, but she married the bastard, and we've made an easy truce.

That doesn't stop me from thinking every hand in a pocket is reaching for a gun. Seeing shadows jump off the walls at me.

I came here today to check on the girl. That part was true. But I also wanted to come back to the place. Face my demons. Make sure I didn't break out in a cold sweat when I was outside the door where I got shot. Didn't act like a fucking pussy just because I took a piece of lead for my family.

Good news: I didn't.

Bad news: I'm not sure what I'm living for.

I mean, I have this second chance.

I didn't die. I'm a dead man walking. So why does my life suddenly feel so fucking empty?

I sit and watch Marissa bustle around, closing the place up. She's young—whole life ahead of her. She's still living for something.

Rather fervently, too.

I suddenly want to know what it is. I want to know all her deep, hidden secrets. Her desires. She darts a few looks at me. I make her nervous. A little self-conscious. But I also make her blush, which makes my dick twitch.

She's beautiful but hasn't figured it out yet. Or downplays it because she doesn't want the attention from men. She's young, smart, and extremely capable. She can't be over twenty-five, and she's been running this place for several years. I seem to recall her grandmother bragging that she went to culinary school.

Lotta good it did her. She's still stuck in her family business, doing the thing that's expected of her.

Just like me.

I get up and leave my plate on the table for her to pick up. If she'd been nicer, I would've brought it up to the counter, especially considering she's trying to close the place, and I'm the asshole still here. But she kept my hundred and played bitch.

So, she can pick up after me.

I stroll to the door, forgetting my swagger for a moment when the scene on the sidewalk replays for me. The smell of my own blood fills my nostrils. I see the face of Ivan, the *bratva* asshole who set us up. The murder in Junior's eyes when he pulled his gun. I hear Paolo's panic when he catches me.

A touch on my arm brings me back. I look down into wide sea-blue eyes.

Just like in the nightmares, only this time her face is soft.

She doesn't say anything for a moment. There's compassion in her gaze. She understands me. "I tried to warn you." Tears pop into her eyes. I wonder if her nightmares are like mine only the other way. Does she see me getting shot over and over again, night after night?

I loop an arm around her waist and pull her in for an embrace. "I know you did."

Fuck, she's enchanting.

"*Thank you,* Marissa." I will her to receive my sincerity.

She hesitates, then brings her arms up around my neck, like one of the dreams. She smells like coffee and sweet cream. I want to lick her skin to see if she tastes as good as she smells.

"I'm glad you made it, Gio. I thought you were dead." Her voice is low and husky. I've been telling myself she's too young for me, and she is, but everything about her registers as a woman who knows what she's about.

"Yeah. Me, too, doll." I drop a kiss on the top of her head and try to ignore the softness of her breasts pressed up against my ribs.

How much I want to kiss her—which isn't like me at all. I'm more into fuck 'em hard and smack their asses when they walk out the door.

Kissing isn't really my gig.

But she saw my death. My near death. The moment

that changed everything. She was part of it. So, I'm imagining some kind of connection.

But that's stupid.

I shouldn't go assigning meaning to things just to try to understand them.

I got shot.

Period.

It's over.

Time to start living again.

❧

Marissa

"WATCH OUT, HENRY'S ON A RAMPAGE," I warn my fellow line chef, Lilah, as I stir the marinara sauce. The temperamental chef's been ripping everyone a new one right and left.

She rolls her caramel-colored eyes. "When is he not?"

"Well, I guess if I were head chef, I might be a temperamental bitch, too," I murmur in an undertone as I pull two stuffed chicken breasts from the oven and plate them. "At least we know what to expect. But you know what I really can't handle anymore?"

Lilah chops asparagus on the diagonal making them all the same exact length. "Arnie?" she whispers back.

"Yeah." Arnie, the *figlio di puttana* sous chef is a leering, groping dickwad who somehow thinks all the women in the kitchen are dying to suck him off. "He patted my ass in the walk-in tonight. *Patted.* It was gross on top of inappropriate."

"Yeah, if you're going to grab-ass, at least make it firm, right?" Lilah grins, dimples creasing her chocolate-brown skin.

I snort. Lilah always makes me laugh. She's the only other young person who works in the kitchen. She started here as a dishwasher when she was sixteen and worked her way up over the last five years. She is definitely one of my favorite people at Michelangelo's.

"Right? It's like creepy molestation versus outright sexual harassment. I don't know—all I know is how violated I feel right now."

"What did you do when it happened?"

"I told him to keep his hands off my ass."

"And let me guess, he laughed like you said something cute."

"Yep. Awesome."

"You should tell Henry."

"Right. Because that will end well. Henry's the one who doesn't seem to think women can do this job. Arnie hired me. I feel like his solution would be to tell me to quit."

I plate a steak and spoon some peppercorn demi-glace over the top.

"Dude, it's *illegal.* Michelangelo's could have a lawsuit on its hands if we report it and they don't do anything."

"Yeah…" And my bosses would also know neither of us have the money to sue. "Maybe I'll just keep a fork in my pocket and next time he comes near me, I'll shove it in his thigh."

Lilah smothers a laugh. "That'll teach him."

Arnie bustles by and she picks up a fork and looks over at him meaningfully.

I duck my head to hide my laugh.

Sadly, I don't get a chance to make use of a fork the rest of the night. By the time we finish cleaning and putting everything away, my feet are killing me and I'm about ready to drop dead, but I'm happy.

I love this job, even with all the bullshit. I like joking with Lilah; I like the excitement of putting plate after plate out with the pressure of perfection. I like working with expensive, gourmet ingredients, making the works of art that Henry dreamed up. I'm always on an adrenaline rush that keeps me going long after closing.

I almost wish the shooting had put Caffè Milano out of business so this was my only job. Maybe it's snobby of me, but I feel like creating fine cuisine in a top-rated restaurant is where I really belong.

But that's selfish. My grandparents raised me and I owe them everything. Caffè Milano is their entire world and they're getting old. My aunt and I are the ones who keep the place going. Even with Aunt Lori working there full-time, I have to fill in more and more the older my grandparents get. Which means until they die, or until my little cousin Mia is old enough to help—providing she can with her hip situation, it has to be my entire world, too.

I DON'T EXPECT to find anyone up at my grandparents' when I get home, but all the lights are on.

14

"Hey, guys," I say when I push the door open.

Both my grandparents and Aunt Lori are awake, sitting around the dining room table, looking like someone just died. My aunt's eyes are red-rimmed and my nonna's mouth is pinched into a tight line, defeat written all over her crumpled face.

"What's going on?" I ask when they just look at me. "What happened?"

"This hospital called this afternoon." My aunt sniffs. "Since we don't have insurance, they refused the surgery for Mia. They said the only way they're going to go through with it as scheduled is if we show up by close of business tomorrow with a check for thirty thousand dollars."

"*What?*" Thirty thousand dollars. That's the going rate for a hip surgery these days. Insane. "Well, that's bullsh… crap."

Aunt Lori tears up again. Her daughter, my eight-year-old cousin, fell on the playground a few months ago and somehow fractured her hip. They did surgery at the time, but the poor kid is still in constant pain and her new surgeon says the screws have come out and are poking her and the whole joint needs to be reconstructed. Again. It's freaking tragic for an eight-year-old to have to go through this shit.

"I know. And I just don't even know what I'm going to tell Mia. We've been trying to get her out of pain for so long."

Now I tear up. It's not right for a kid to be in constant pain. To not be able to play with her friends, or even walk around her school. All because our health care system in this country is so broken.

Working at Caffè Milano, my aunt and I both make too much to qualify for Medicaid but we can't afford health insurance. At least my grandparents can get Medicare.

I sink into a chair and kick off my shoes. "We'll figure this out," I promise.

I don't know how or when I became the person this family looks to for answers, but at some point, I did. My mom abandoned me as a kid, so this is my nuclear family: my elderly grandparents, my aunt—who, like my mom, got pregnant young and out of wedlock—her daughter Mia and me. We stick together and look after one another. We're family, and we figure things out.

"How?" Aunt Lori wails. "How are we going to come up with thirty thousand dollars by tomorrow?"

Sometimes it just takes the right phrasing of a question to discover the answer.

It suddenly becomes clear as day. Inevitable, even.

The Tacones have cash. Stacks of it. All there for the asking.

All I have to do is sell my soul.

Fuck.

I don't say anything in front of my grandparents because I know it would kill them.

"Tomorrow I'll see if I can get a loan. I'm sure the bank will give us something with the cafe as collateral."

Aunt Lori's too distraught to notice my lie. Too desperate to grasp on to any answer. "You think so?"

"Definitely. I'll get it figured out tomorrow. I promise."

Mia needs help. Time to put on my big girl panties and do what has to be done.

~

Gio

I WAKE to the sound of my own shout, the, *No!* echoing off my bedroom walls, Marissa's horror-stricken face burnt into my retinas, those bluish green-colored eyes bright with tears.

Fuck.

I throw the sheet off my sweat-drenched body and get up, my side pulling with a dull ache. The scar tissue is getting stiffer every day.

Desiree—Junior's bride, the nurse who saved my life — says I need to get the fascia worked out. She wants me to see a physical therapist or some other shit, but that bullet hole is evidence to the crime Junior committed, killing those *bratva* bastards who shot me. So yeah, not happening. I stick to my morning run and lifting weights in my home gym.

I stand shirtless in the window of my apartment and look out at Lake Michigan. Sailboats cut through the water, picturesque as a fucking painting. Maybe I should learn to sail.

The thought falls like a brick, like all thoughts for my life. For my future.

Meh.

I'm living the goddamn dream here. Penthouse apartment right on Lake Shore Drive, lavish furnishings, the black Mercedes G-wagon in the garage.

I was already pimping it before I got a second chance

at life. So why am I the least grateful fuck in Chicago? I should be waking up every day thanking my lucky stars for all I have to live for.

Except that's just it.

There's nothing to live for.

Not even the glory of business anymore.

I'm not saying I miss it. The violence, the danger. The intrigue. But there was a certain adrenaline rush that came with every interaction. The thrill of taking care of business. Watching money multiply. Loaning it. Collecting it.

Junior shut down a lot of the business after I got shot. Although that may be more about becoming a husband and daddy again than about almost losing me. Not that I think he didn't suffer over what happened. I know he did. Does.

His job was always to protect me, from the time I was born. And he has. Even when that meant shielding me from the judgment of our own father. He and Paolo were the badasses, and I was the finesse. I did the smooth talking when it was needed. Played good cop, not that we ever played cops.

I wander into the living room, still in my boxer briefs and sit down at the baby grand in the corner. My fingers move over the keys automatically, the muscle memory there without thought. I still have my music. Too bad it's not enough.

My phone rings beside me, and I stop playing and pick it up. It's the phone number I use for women, only I haven't been with a woman since the accident.

Marissa. I gave her the number before I left the other day.

Never expected her to use it.

I pick up. "This is Gio."

"Gio, hi. It's Marissa. From Caffè Milano?" She sounds nervous.

"Everything okay, doll?"

"Um, yeah. Well, I need to talk to you. Can I meet you somewhere? Not at the cafe."

I don't know what I hoped. That she had the nerve to ask me out. Or was calling to tell me again that she's glad I'm alive.

That she knows I dream about her every night.

Of course not. There's only one reason I get a call like this.

And I fucking hate the way it makes me feel.

"Sure, Marissa. Why don't you come to my home office?" My dick gets hard as I give her the address to my apartment, even though I know that's not how things are going to go down.

Just the idea of having her here gets me chubby, though.

I hang up and give my cock a rough squeeze. Down, boy. This is business, not pleasure.

Too fucking bad.

CHAPTER 2

$\mathcal{M}$*arissa*

GIO LIVES RIGHT on Lake Shore Drive in what must be a million-dollar townhouse on the top floor. I took the L in and walked the rest of the way in my high heels. I have blisters by the time I reach his building, and I'm cursing everything about my plan.

I dug in the back of my closet for a silk blouse, pencil skirt and these cursed stilettos, but now I'm wondering what the hell I was thinking. Am I here to sell myself to Gio? Dress up like a pretty piece of meat, flirt a little and get thirty grand?

I guess it's better than my alternative, which is to sign the cafe back over to the Tacones, which would absolutely kill my grandfather. I don't even know if the place is worth that much, anyway. We don't own the real estate. I'm not even sure if a bank would give us a loan against our business.

It's a beautiful fall morning, but I'm icy cold when the doorman opens the door for me and takes my name to call up to Gio.

This is for Mia, I keep chanting to myself.

In the elevator, though, I lose my nerve.

Gio's going to want the cafe. I can't give it to him. I can't. My grandparents wouldn't think it's worth it, not even for Mia.

Thinking he might give me the money for something else—for me? Was that the idea in the back of my head? It's—ludicrous. And I don't want to resort to begging or whoring myself out.

There must be another way.

And there is.

I have dirt on the Tacones. I can leverage it. They already paid us hush money when they overpaid for the repairs to the place after the shooting. They can pay a little more.

Stiffening my spine, I walk out of the elevator with my head high and ring Gio's doorbell.

He answers, dressed to the nines, as usual, in a suit that probably costs more than a car, smelling of soap and aftershave.

He gives me a cool, assessing glance, taking in my outfit and expression, then steps back from the door and ushers me in. "Welcome, Marissa."

The apartment is huge with a wall of windows looking out over Lake Michigan and a black baby grand in one corner.

"Do you play piano?" The stupid question tumbles out of my mouth before I can stop it. I'm nervous—saying anything to fill the space. Of course he doesn't play piano. Some decorator probably put that in here.

But he surprises me with a "yeah".

"Really?" Now I'm genuinely interested. A mafioso who plays piano? Unexpected.

"Really, doll. Surprised?" There's a challenge in his tone, and it occurs to me that he might have had to fight that same stereotype his whole life.

"Um…"

"My office is through here." He's all business, which is more disappointing than I care to admit. But this is business. And I need to follow through on my plan.

For Mia.

He leads me to the office, decorated in red leather and mahogany wood. Masculine and comfortable in that rich gentleman sort of style.

"Have a seat." He indicates the padded leather chair across from his desk and settles opposite me.

I sit and cross my legs like a lady. Fight and fail to swallow. My tongue tangles in my mouth.

"What can I do for you, Marissa?" Everything about him this morning is cool and manicured. So different from the casual charming demeanor he had at the cafe.

I clear my throat. "The shooting had a big effect on business," I say, which is a lie. It happened in the evening, when almost no one is around, and the Tacones paid for immediate clean up and repairs, so we were only closed one day.

The way Gio raises one brow tells me he knows I'm

bullshitting. I also sense his disapproval. Like he knows where this is going and doesn't like it.

I rush on. "We require another payment of at least thirty grand to make things right."

Gio doesn't say a word. Nothing shows on his face. Even his eyes—usually so beautifully warm are dead.

My heart pounds so loudly I swear he can hear it. Sweat trickles down my ribs.

"What for?" he says.

"I'm sorry?"

"What's the money for?"

I'm so breathless I can barely speak. But I force the words across my lips. "To keep us quiet," I say.

Gio's mouth tightens.

"I told the cops it was the Russians. But I could call them—"

Gio holds up a finger to interrupt. "Don't fucking say it." His gaze is black as night. "Seriously. Nobody black-mails a Tacone and walks away."

I choke on my breath.

Blackmail. Yes, I guess that is what I just attempted. And now I am so fucked.

Did he just tell me I'm dead? Will he shoot me right here? Or drive me out to the woods and make me dig my own grave?

I stand up from the chair and start toward the door. "You can't… I'm… the feds know I'm here," I blurt. "I'm wearing a wire."

"Don't touch that door." His command rings out with steely authority. I freeze. Maybe he has a gun pointed at my head.

Gio reaches me at the door. He catches my wrists and pins them behind my back with one hand and flattens me against the thick, expensive wood. With the other, he burrows his fingers into my French twist and tugs my head back. "Wearing a wire." His voice drips with disbelief.

I try to answer, but only an unintelligible sound escapes my lips.

"Well, I guess I'd better check." His hand slides across my belly, inside my blouse.

The moment it does, the air electrifies between us. Changes.

He knows without a shadow of a doubt I'm bluffing. His touch sears my skin even though he barely ghosts across the surface. He holds me captive as he checks inside both bra cups, between my breasts, down my back. "Nothing here." His voice sounds deeper than before. Not quite as controlled or angry.

He pulls the zipper down on my skirt and it falls to the floor at my feet. I'm wearing pale pink thigh highs that match my panties and bra.

He tsks. "Was this really your plan? Put on grown up clothes, show me a little cleavage and these pretty legs and then threaten me? Very bad move, Marissa."

"I-I'm sorry, Mr. Tacone."

"Our families go way back. We're allies, babygirl. All you had to do was ask for the money and it would've been yours. Instead you point a gun at me."

"I-I don't have a gun."

His chuckle is dark and rumbles through my limbs, making them even weaker. "Metaphor, angel."

"Oh." *Oh.* That's all I can think to say? I'm going to

have to think faster if I'm going to dig my way out of this disaster.

"Why would you threaten me, Marissa? You have to know how easy it would be for me to wipe you and your entire family out of existence. You've seen with your own eyes what we're capable of."

My body goes rigid. Ice cold. "You can't kill me." I'm choking on my own spit.

He laughs again, but switches his hand from my hair to my nape and presses me against the door, my cheek flattening with the steady pressure. "You sure about that?"

His other hand starts swiftly roaming over the back of my panties, inside the waistband, between my legs.

Cold turns into the hot flush of embarrassment. He gives my ass a light slap. "No wire. But we already knew that. You're a horrible liar, Marissa."

I choke on the tears in my throat. "But you had to strip search me anyway?"

His searching hand rests lightly at my hip. He strokes it down the side of my thigh and up to my waist. "That wasn't a strip search. You still have clothes on. But I'd be happy to comply if that's what you're going for."

"You're sick," I bite out.

He slaps my ass again, this time hard. "And you're in a world of trouble." He pulls me off the door, and I step out of the skirt at my feet before he spins me around and marches me to the leather chair and pushes me into it.

"I'm disappointed in you, Marissa." He stares down at me with dark, glittering eyes. "Like, heartbreakingly disappointed."

I rub my lips together, heart beating as fast as a hummingbird's.

He cocks his head to the side. "Was it pride?"

"What?"

"That kept you from just asking?" He trails a finger over the cap sleeve of my blouse thoughtfully. "Feminism?"

He really wants to know. I think I genuinely offended him by not asking for the favor. He wanted to be that guy who granted it. Wanted to be sugar daddy to me and I denied him the pleasure.

Why did I? He's right. It would've been easy. I knew he would've given me the money. I guess I just wanted some measure of control in this interaction. Which is like the gazelle trying to dominate the lion.

I swallow past the band of dread around my throat and nod. "Something like that," I admit.

He leans against his desk, facing me, arms folded casually over his chest. He's downright debonair in his expensive suit pants and button-down shirt, open at the throat. He sweeps a cool glance down my body, making me acutely aware of the fact that I'm in my panties, with the full length of my legs on display for him.

"How's that working out for you?"

Hot tears spill down my cheeks. He pushes away from the desk and wipes one with his thumb. "You don't need to cry. A guy like me might let anything slide when it comes to a woman as beautiful as you. Especially considering our family history."

Might.

He might let anything slide.

And that's when I admit to myself that I knew that all along. I knew he wouldn't kill me. I know I wouldn't get the control I so desperately wanted. I knew it would come to this. Him demanding sexual favors from me.

And the stupid part of it all is that the idea isn't abhorrent because he disgusts me. Or that I don't want to have sex with him.

Because honestly?

I do.

He's sexy as hell.

It's because I'm afraid I'll like it.

That, and I don't want to belong to the devil himself.

"I'm not having sex with you," I blurt.

I think he's going to scowl or worse, tell me coolly why I am. Instead, his smile stretches wide. "Thanks for the clarification, doll, but I'm not interested. I don't have to force or pay for sex, babygirl."

My face flushes hot, even as a similar tingle puckers my nipples and pools in my belly. I still feel his hands all over my body. Everywhere those large, rough palms traveled over my bare skin.

He puts a finger under my chin and tips my face up to his. "But what am I going to do with you? That's the question."

I blink rapidly at the tears forming on my lashes.

"How much do you need?"

I go still. Is he going to give me the money? After I royally fucked this up? "Thirty thousand." My voice cracks.

"What for?"

I gulp. "My little cousin needs a surgery. She's scheduled for it Monday, but insurance refused to pay and the hospital called and said if they don't get a check by close of business today, they won't do it."

I swear Gio looks a little sad. "That's all you had to tell me, you know."

Heaviness descends down to my belly. Like I'm taking his disappointment in me to heart. Which is stupid.

"You didn't have to show the legs or the cleavage. You didn't have to *fucking blackmail me*." He raises his voice on the last three words, and I see the Tacone temper that I expected.

The trembling starts up again. "I'm sorry," I whisper.

He folds his arms over his chest, his gaze suddenly hard. "You should be."

He walks behind his desk and takes a painting off the wall. Behind it lies a safe. He opens it, pulls out three stacks of hundred-dollar bills, and tosses them into my lap.

Gio

I SHOULDN'T BE SO butthurt. I'm the guy people come to when they need money. Usually, if they have nothing to offer, there's begging and pleading. The promise of any favor I demand. Threats are far less common.

Marissa was beyond stupid to go there with me.

Still, it sours everything for me. Doesn't make me any less hard for her, but it sours things.

Here I'd been attaching some mythical importance to

her—the girl in every nightmare. I sensed her attraction to me. Wondered if maybe it all meant something.

Something bigger.

Like my second chance has something to do with her.

Fucking ha.

She needs thirty grand just like every other sorry ass applicant for a Tacone loan. And instead of asking, she comes in and demands it with a threat.

Yeah, I'm still pissed. I want to slap her ass red for it.

As if she reads my mind, she looks up at me, not touching the bundles of money I threw in her lap. "I'm sorry. I really fucked this up. Fucked up with you." Her lips tremble, but she meets my gaze with courage. I enjoy the way her chest rises and falls, causing the opening in her silk blouse to shift over her breasts. "I can't believe you're still giving me the money."

I perch on the edge of my desk again. It's a power position. I get to lounge casually while still looming over her. "I woulda given it to you in a heartbeat, doll. No collateral but your grandma's fucking cannoli. But now I'm kinda pissed."

She nods. "I know." A tear slides from the outer corner of one eye but her face remains stoic. She's brave, I give her that. Stupid, but she's got balls. "I was going to just come and ask. I don't know why I put on the clothes." She tugs the blouse down like it might cover her panties if she tries hard enough.

I like her bared to me like this. Like it way too fucking much.

"But then I got scared. I was afraid you'd take owner-ship of Caffè Milano, like your dad did. It took my grandfather forty years to pay him off. Or I don't know—maybe he never did and you and your brothers just let it go when your dad went..." She trails off like she's afraid of offending me.

"To jail?"

She nods.

I consider her, trying to remember the business end of the deal. Milano's was just always our haunt, for as long as I can remember. I never thought about how or why. Junior would probably know.

"My father often structured loans to keep men permanently under his thumb." Might as well call a spade a spade. "He probably made it impossible to pay off so we could use Milano's as our headquarters."

She grows pale, like this news is even worse than what she'd imagined. Clearly the old man has kept her sheltered.

"So, you don't want me to have Milano's." I shrug. "I am fond of the place, but it's all right. I didn't see myself serving espresso and wiping tables anyway. We can work out a different deal."

She stares up at me, her blue-green gaze wary. "What kind of deal?"

"I don't know." I tilt my head. "Didn't you go to culinary school? I could use a personal chef around here."

The relief that ripples through her is immediately apparent by the way her posture straightens and her eyes widen. "Oh my God, I can do that. I mean, *yes*." She actually seems excited by the idea. A woman who loves her craft. "I can prepare meals for you and drop them off. A couple days at a time. Or a full week. Whatever you want, Mr. Tacone."

"First off, you're gonna call me Gio or we're gonna to have a problem. I mean *another* problem."

Her lips quirk. There. It's funny how relieved I am to see her relax.

"Secondly, I wasn't thinking drop-offs. I was thinking you'd come in here—with or without the tight little skirt—and cook in my kitchen." In fact, my cock gets hard thinking about it.

Some of the tension returns. "I can't. I mean, maybe one night a week. But I work full-time at a restaurant and at Milano's every other minute."

"Hard worker." I'm not surprised. She may have screwed up this meeting, but she's got capable written all over her. "Okay. One night a week you cook dinner for me and leave my prepared meals for the week. I'll deduct five hundred a week from your tab and give you cash for groceries."

She gathers the money on her lap—it's the first time she's touched it—and stands. "Are you serious?"

I brace myself for her gratitude. I don't know—I almost prefer her prickly and throwing shade to moments like this. Where she shows me everything in the depths of those innocent eyes. She puts her arms around me like she did the other night at the cafe and leans in for a hug.

I don't read too much into it—she's Italian, like me. We touch. We kiss. We hug. But she's in her panties and these fucking thigh-highs that make my dick harder than stone and she definitely feels my appreciation.

Her breath catches and there's this moment of hesitation.

She doesn't jerk away. She goes still.

The old Gio woulda had her on her back by now. I'd lay her out on my desk, spread those legs and pound her hard, and all the time she'd be thanking me for the fuck and the money.

New Gio thinks too much.

Or maybe it's just because it's Marissa. The girl from the nightmares.

She said she's not having sex with me. I know I could make her willing. I know she wants it, even.

But I can't take the weight of any new shit on my conscience. Fucking the Milano girl after what just passed between us would be questionable. She would go for it, but she'd hate me tomorrow. So, I force myself to unwind my arm from around her back, and I deliver a light slap to her ass.

"I'm still pissed."

It was the right thing to do. She gets her confidence back and flashes me a flirtatious smile, dumping the money on my desk. "You won't be after you taste the food I cook you."

"Confident. I like that."

She retrieves her skirt and pulls it on.

Because I can't resist getting close to her again, I step up behind her, bat her hands away and zip it up.

I can't fucking wait to taste the food she cooks me.

Finally, a reason to live.

∾

Marissa

GOOSEBUMPS RISE ON MY ARMS.

I've never had a guy dress me before. There's something so intimate to Gio closing the zipper of my skirt—more intimate, even, than the strip search. Than standing in front of him with my skirt off.

It's like something a married guy does with his wife. In the movies, though. Only in the movies. I don't know; I only have my grandparents as examples, but I feel like married couples become way too practical for dressing each other.

I'm giddy now. All my fears and anxieties morphed into something exciting. The relief of paying for Mia's surgery, mingles with the anticipation of showing off my cooking skills, all woven together with a heavy layer of sexual tension.

"Come on, I'll drive you to the hospital." Gio's still right behind me, his deep, gruff voice doing crazy things to my core.

I turn, surprised. "You will?"

He arches a cocky brow. The frightening mafioso is gone now and charming Gio is back. "You think I'm going to let you toddle out in those heels? You barely made it here."

My face grows warm. "You noticed that, huh?"

Gio's eyes crinkle up and he holds out a hand. His lanky form is relaxed; he oozes confidence and ease. "Which hospital?"

I hesitate for a moment before putting my hand in his. This is it.

I'm joining with the devil.

My small palm slides over his larger one and he closes his fingers.

I clear my throat. "St. Francis, but I have to stop at the bank to get a cashier's check."

"All right. Let's go."

"THANKS FOR THE RIDE," I murmur when we pull into the hospital lot. The crisp cashier's check is in my hand, but Gio doesn't let me out in front; he parks and gets out.

I thought the ride was exceptionally generous, especially considering the way things went down between us. But now I wonder what his game is.

"Are you making sure I didn't lie about what I need the money for?"

One corner of his lips quirk in that knowing smile. "You didn't lie." He walks around his beautiful Mercedes G-wagon to my side and settles a hand on my lower back.

"You don't need to come in," I tell him. I still can't figure it out, which makes me uneasy.

"I'm coming in."

This is the part that worries me. A Tacone does what he wants. There's no asking. No negotiations. And I just opened the door and let him firmly back into our lives.

I stop mulishly. "Why, Gio?"

"Because I want to, doll. Stop being so ungracious."

The words roll out easily, but I get the sense I offended him again.

But that doesn't make sense.

I start walking again, sneaking glances at him as we go.

"What?" he demands when we get in an elevator up to the finance floor.

I shake my head quickly.

He exhales, like he's conceding something. "I'm here to watch your back, Marissa. You carry a lot of weight for your family. Least I can do is drive your ass to the hospital and go in with you to make sure it gets done right."

I blink back the heat that sears my eyeballs. Just having someone acknowledge the weight on my shoulders comes as a relief, but to also hear that Gio Tacone actually does care about me and my family—as he's been professing—comes as a shock. Guilt for all my mistrust, for my attempted blackmail and all my bitchiness floods through me. I check to see if my mouth is hanging open.

"I know, shocker." He shoves his hands in his pockets and leans a shoulder against the elevator wall. "And you thought I was incapable of doing anything nice."

"I didn't—" but I stop the protest, because he's right.

The elevator stops and we get out. I square my shoulders and stride toward the business office. I'm glad I wore the skirt and heels now, because they lend me confidence. I feel strangely strong and sexy. Is it because I have Gio at my back? Or because that's how he sees me, and I sense his appreciation? I shoot him a sidelong glance and he returns it, one corner of his mouth turning up like he's sex on a stick.

Funny, how I do want to reward him with sex now. I guess that's the difference. I didn't want it to be something he took from me. Or demanded. Now he's earned it.

Oh, lordy. Why am I even thinking about sex with Gio? Not happening. Bad idea. He's a player and a mobster. Not the man I want to tango with.

We get to the business office and I slide the check across the desk. "I'm here to pay for Mia Milano's surgery." I lift my chin. One word and she's going to get an earful about what I think about this hospital and their blackmailing techniques.

She types in Mia's name and clicks on her computer for a few minutes. "Okay, your total is $32,784.59."

I look at the check. Why hadn't I considered it might be *more* than thirty grand? "This is thirty thousand. I'll put the rest on my credit card."

"No." Gio shoves his hand inside his jacket pocket and produces a huge wad of cash. He counts out twenty-eight hundred-dollar bills. "This will cover it."

I refuse to show my gratitude for it, or let on how much seeing a handsome man throw down that amount of cash without blinking an eye affects me. I just take the money and slide it over, like dealing with such a sum is something I do every day.

"We don't usually accept a large amount of cash. I'll have to call my supervisor to make sure we can take this."

"You do that," Gio says. On another man it might sound rude or condescending, but this is Gio, so the clerk thinks he's flirting. She blushes and smiles at him with the phone to her ear. A few minutes later, she hangs up. "We can take it." She counts it all and calls for a security guy to deposit it. "You're all set, then. I'll let the doctor know you're paid up and Mia's surgery can go on as scheduled tomorrow."

"Thank you," I say tightly and turn away before I go off on her. It's not her fault this country has a broken healthcare system.

We walk back to the elevator without saying a word. Only when we're in it do I turn and look Gio full in the face. "You'll add the extra to my tab, I presume?"

He purses his lips, like he finds me amusing, but doesn't speak for a moment. "It's on me, doll."

That shouldn't get me wet. We're not on a date. He didn't just pay for dinner. In fact, I know from my grandfather's dealings with Arturo Tacone that nothing comes free with these guys. But there's some stupid biology involved. Sexy alpha male as wealthy, powerful provider. Hormones are flooding my system. My internal biology is screaming *yes! Pick this one!*

Silly, silly ovaries. Stop dropping eggs. We're not hooking up with this guy. Definitely not having his babies.

Still, I find myself locked in his gaze, mirroring that amused, secret smile he wears.

The elevator opens and I snap back to reality. "I can find my own way home. Thank you, Gio."

"Nah. I'm driving you home, angel. No arguments."

No arguments. He's bossy as hell. Which also shouldn't be a turn-on.

"I live with my grandparents," I blurt, in case he's thinking I'm going to have sex with him when we get home.

Amusement flickers over his face. He opens my door for me.

"I don't want them to know about this," I tell him.

He goes still. "All right," he says slowly.

I climb into the seat to keep from saying more, not wanting to offend him. And I know by now that he does ruffle, despite the casual debonair attitude he wears so well.

He walks around and gets in the driver side. "You didn't sign over the cafe. You're just cooking food."

"I know, but they wouldn't like it," I admit.

"They have a problem with me?" he demands.

Dammit. He took offense. I can't help but admire his directness, though. He's a man accustomed to getting to the bottom of things. Apparently not just with his fists.

"Not with you, specifically," I hedge. Which is true. "But I didn't tell them I was going to you for the money. They'd be worried about accruing debt to the Tacones again."

"It's not the Tacones, it's me," Gio says, like that clears everything up. "The Family doesn't own the marker. I won't put it in our books, okay? It's just between you and me."

I'm wet again. I don't know why his willingness to extend kindness to me has such an effect, but it does.

"So, you won't tell my grandparents?"

"Nah."

"Promise?"

"*Lo prometto.*" He takes a hand off the wheel and holds it up like he's swearing to a judge. His sexy black

SUV darts through traffic, his driving prowess no less impressive than everything else he does.

I sit back in the comfortable leather seat and allow myself to believe everything's going to be all right.

To believe I can trust Gio Tacone and that I didn't just sign my soul over to the devil.

CHAPTER 3

 io

"YOU LOOK DIFFERENT," my older brother Paolo says to me. We're at my ma's house for Sunday dinner. Our oldest brother Junior and his new wife Desiree are in the kitchen making dinner because Ma's getting too old to cook for all of us. Plus, she's holding Junior and Desiree's baby, Santo Tacone the III, making a crazy fuss over him.

There's still a touch of wonder in the baby thing for all of us. Junior lost his toddler in a drowning accident ten years ago and shut down emotionally. Until this year, we hadn't had another child in the family. Now we have five, if you count my sister's two Russian stepchildren and Desiree's son Jasper.

"You look like the same *stronzo*," I say to Paolo. As

41

the brother just two years older than me, he thinks his job in life is to bust my balls.

What the fuck does he mean I look different?

He's staring at me avidly, like my nose is in a new place or something.

"What?"

"I don't know. You look better. More like yourself."

It's Marissa.

I want to deny the whisper of truth. I already know I'm attaching way too much importance to this girl.

She happens to be the unfortunate female stuck in a loop of my nightmares. And she also happens to owe me thirty grand, which she'll be paying back in a way that I'm far too excited about. But whatever. As long as I don't assign meaning to it, I should be happy anything has me excited.

So, I guess Paolo's right. I'm more myself.

Except I don't know who the fuck *myself* even is anymore.

I keep that existential malaise to myself, though. The last thing I need is Junior or Paolo messing with my life to try to fix me.

Italian families. They're way too fucking interfering.

I head over to my ma's piano and sit down and play *Get Lucky* by Daft Punk. I know Jasper will recognize it. He runs over and stands beside me to listen.

"Play it again, Uncle Gio," he demands when I finish.

"No, it's time to eat," Desiree tells him. She raises her voice to call all of us. "Dinner's ready."

I watch her bustle around, pouring water into everyone's glasses. She has this capable way of serving without being the slightest bit servile. A spitfire Puerto Rican American, she was our mother's in-home nurse before Junior kidnapped her to nurse me back to the land of the living. She was the only nurse my mother didn't steamroll and she's easily won all our respect and love.

Junior carries in a casserole dish of stuffed baked ziti and sets it on the table before sitting in our father's chair at the head.

Desiree takes baby Santo from my mother's arms and sits him on her lap, where he starts grabbing things from the table. She scoots breakables away and hands him a spoon. "Gio, you look good."

"See?" Paolo says. "That's what I told him. What happened? You get laid?"

"Paolo," Ma scolds. "There are children present and you're sitting at my dinner table."

"Sorry, Ma."

But now the whole table's looking at me. "I'm feeling good, that's all." I wave off the attention. Our mother never knew about me getting shot, so I'm purposely vague.

"Good. That's good." A trace of worry is in Junior's gaze. There's a lot of shit I could blame him for, but not taking me to the hospital when I got shot isn't one of them. He doesn't need that on his conscience. I know he did what he had to do to protect all of us. And I lived.

If anything, I resent that he's moved on. He shut down the Family business to settle down with Desiree. And I'm left holding my dick.

And I don't know what the fuck Paolo's doing. I think he's still running a side business on his own, which none of us ever mention.

But I guess we're free to do that. We're grown men with millions of dollars each, thanks to the Family's investment in Nico's casino.

"Gio and Paolo, when are you going to give me grand-children?" Ma starts in.

"Don't count on it," Paolo says. "Not from me, anyway. But who knows, maybe Gio will give up his playboy ways now."

"What do you mean *now*?" Ma says.

Junior shoots Paolo a warning look.

Paolo plays it off with a shrug. "Now that four of our siblings have taken the fall."

"The fall? Real nice, Paolo," Desiree shoots from across the table with an eye roll. She hands him the basket of bread, though, which he was trying to reach.

I don't desire a wife and kids.

At least I never did. Even watching my brothers and sister find love didn't change that for me. Although it did add to my inner crisis. Like, why the fuck *don't* I want that?

Shouldn't I want it?

The only thing is, I'm suddenly picturing Marissa here at this table. She'd be serving her gourmet food, giving Paolo shit right along with Desiree.

What would she look like pregnant?

I shake my head, blinking. Trying to push away the goddess-gorgeous image I have of her in a flowing white gown, hair tumbling over her shoulder and a swollen belly.

I must be fucking nuts.

She's not the missing meaning in my life. I need to stop assigning that kind of bullshit importance to her.

She's a barely legal chef who owes me money.

End of story.

Marissa

I TAKE Lilah's arm and tug her into the walk-in with me. "Arnie grabbed my boob and I didn't have the damn fork on me. Actually, he *honked* it, like a sixth grader who wants to get kneed in the balls."

"Did you? Knee him in the balls?"

I groan, slumping. "I actually tried, but he was too quick. Who do you think I should tell? Henry or Michael?" Michael is the owner. He's pretty hands-off with the kitchen, leaving all the hiring, firing and management to Henry and Arnie.

"Maybe Michael. He's the one with a liability here. You know what you should do? Go home tonight and then call him tomorrow before anyone's here. That way Arnie and Henry won't see you going over their heads."

Arnie pokes his head in the walk-in, then grins and saunters in with a broad grin. "What's going on, girls? I thought you'd already gone home."

"We're just leaving." I push forcibly past him, feeling Lilah right behind me. We grab our jackets and head out. *Ugh.*

"Call tomorrow," Lilah says firmly as we part ways. "Promise?"

"Yeah," I say, although I still haven't made up my

mind. I like this job so much, I'm not sure I want to risk fucking things up. Besides, Arnie's not a real danger. He's an annoyance, not a rapist.

At least I hope.

I walk toward the train station.

At first, I don't notice the car that pulls out, but when it drives slowly beside me and the window comes down, I look over. Only because of my thoughts about Arnie, I imagine for a minute it might be him.

But that's dumb. It's a beautiful black SUV. One I recognize immediately.

Gio's.

I stop.

"Get in the car."

My heart's still beating fast. I can't decide if it's because this looks like the start of every deadly mafia scene I've ever seen in the movies or if it's because of what Gio does to my body.

Either way, I'm not getting in. I start walking again. "No, thanks."

I sense Gio's annoyance through the open window as he eases off the brake and follows me.

"Marissa. I'm gonna drive you home. That's all. Get in the fucking car."

I stop again. "What are you even doing here?"

We'd exchanged a few texts about which night I'm coming to his place and the details. He asked where I work and I told him. It definitely wasn't an invitation.

"I was trying out the food. Wanted to see where you worked."

I raise my brows. "We closed an hour ago."

"Yeah. I was at the bar having a drink. Now I'm leaving, and I see you walking alone. I don't like it."

I'm not sure I buy his story. Feels to me like he was sitting in his car waiting for me. It's a little scary, considering his profession.

"I walk alone every night, Gio. I'm fine." I turn my collar up against the fall chill and walk on.

"Marissa." His voice bites out, sharp with command. He's a man used to getting his way. Used to having his orders obeyed. The sound of his voice does something to me, even though I don't want to let him have power over me. "Get in the fucking car."

"I'm good, Gio." I try to keep my voice light.

"You know I can make you, right?"

That does something unexpected to me. My reaction isn't fear. It's heat. Liquid lava pooling between my legs. A clenching in my pussy.

I turn to face him for the first time. "You'd probably like that."

The annoyance on his face morphs into a twisted smirk —the one that melts panties across the city. "You might, too, angel. Wanna try?"

My face grows warm, but tingles spread across my skin. "What are you going to do?" My voice sounds ridiculously husky.

His grin widens. "Get in the car before I smack your ass pink."

My ass clenches and tingles in response, the memory of his spanks at his apartment rushing back.

He's definitely not the butt-pat type like Arnie. He's at the opposite end of harassment. The kind you want to

47

experience again and again.

I pull open the door and climb inside. Whether it's because I'm not willing to find out if he'd follow through or because I want him to, I'm not sure.

"Not sure if I'm happy you obeyed or disappointed I don't get to follow through." He voices my exact thoughts.

I sense heat flush across my chest and up my neck. "I think you've seen enough of my ass already," I say primly.

His chuckle is dark and wicked. "Oh, not nearly, angel. But this is just a ride home. You don't have to hang on to the seat belt like it's the only thing keeping you safe from me."

I steal a sidelong glance at him, devouring his breathtaking beauty for a hot minute.

"How did your cousin's surgery go?"

"Good. Thank you. She's recovering like a champ." Gratitude to Gio warms my chest. Not just for the money, but for his continued interest—helping me at the hospital, asking now. I steal one more glance. "Why are you really here, Gio?"

He shrugs and returns his gaze to the road. After a moment of silence, he says, "Honest truth?"

I twist to face him.

"You want the God's honest truth?"

My heart picks up speed. I sense something big coming, but can't imagine what it would be. "Yes." I sound breathless.

"You're in my nightmares, angel. The ones where I get shot? Sometimes you get shot, too."

I stifle a gasp.

"I guess because you were there when it happened.

And so now I feel attached to you. And it's stupid, but sometimes I'm afraid it's a warning. Like I'm supposed to make sure nothing happens to you."

I sit in shocked silence, prickles raising the hairs on my arms. Of all the confessions I expected—and I expected zero, but still—it wouldn't be this one.

"Th-that's why you came to Milano's? To check on me?"

He gives a single nod.

"Is that why you loaned me the money?"

He shrugs. "I'm sure I would've loaned it anyway. But yeah. It feels more significant."

I'm stunned.

Gio Tacone is superstitious. Or religious. Or whatever. Which I guess makes sense, considering he had a near-death experience.

It changes everything I feel about the man. Well, maybe not everything, but a lot. His motives aren't sinister.

And it's stupid, but knowing he's assigned meaning to my presence in his nightmares makes me feel special. Knowing he thinks he's supposed to protect me gives me secret strength.

I reach out and touch his arm. "All this time, I've been trying to figure out what you really wanted from me. Why you were being so kind. I thought it might be a trick."

He shakes his head. "No trick. But don't go assuming this makes me a nice guy," he warns, pulling on to my grandparents' street. "I'm not. I'm just… trying to get rid of the bad dreams."

I smile softly. It's on the tip of my tongue to suggest a

therapist instead of following me around, but then I don't really want that.

I kind of like knowing the playboy Gio Tacone is semi-obsessed with me. At least with keeping me safe.

It's like I have my own personal superhero. The dark kind who wields a shit ton of power but has done many bad things with it. Or is he actually the supervillain teetering on the edge of redemption?

Either way, I'm so freaking turned on by that.

He pulls up at the curb and I lean over, giving him a kiss on the cheek. "Thanks, Gio. You're a true prince."

He snorts. "Watch it, angel. I'll disabuse you of that notion in seconds flat."

I grin. It's a wicked grin. The flirty kind I've never worn before. "Can't wait."

Oh God, did I say that? Too late to take it back. I close the door on the surprise flaring in his eyes and hustle away to my grandparents' door.

Gio Tacone. My dark prince.

I freaking love it.

CHAPTER 4

 io

I told Marissa to call when she got to the L station. That I'd pick her up so she wasn't walking alone at night.

And somehow, I knew she wouldn't.

Whether it's because she's stubborn and independent or whether it's because she's testing my threat to spank her ass, I'm not sure. I definitely noticed how she turned to hot syrup and got flirty with me when I said it.

Either way, when the doorman calls up to say she's downstairs, I'm pissed off and turned on all at once. "Send her up," I tell him and stand in my doorway, arms folded across my chest.

The first thing I see when the elevator doors open is the skirt and heels. Cue the soundtrack: *She's Got Legs.* And she definitely knows how to use them.

51

My cock gets harder than stone as I watch her toss that caramel-colored hair and strut into my apartment.

She brought a crate on a handcart, which I take from her and wheel in after the customary two cheek air kisses.

"I asked you to call me from the station," I remind her the moment I shut the door.

"I wanted to walk." She breezes past me into my kitchen, like she knows full well I'll follow with the groceries. She probably knows I'm watching her ass, too, based on the way she's swishing it. As soon as we're in the kitchen I leave the cart and crowd up behind her, pushing her hips up to the granite countertop.

"Angel, you must've misunderstood," I rumble in her ear as I catch both her wrists and pin them behind her back.

She gasps, but says nothing, her quickened breath the evidence of her excitement.

I give her ass a hard slap—punishment hard—and she jerks a bit. "See, in this situation, I'm like your employer. You're working for me." Another hard slap, this time on the other cheek.

She shifts on her heels, wobbling slightly.

"When I give you directions, I expect them to be followed, angel." One more slap. "Or there will be consequences." I rub the last place I spanked, letting the slippery fabric slide over the luscious curve of her ass.

I reach past her to pull a wooden spoon out of the crock of utensils. I slide it under her nose. "Disobey me again, angel, and the skirt comes off."

I allow myself one more rub, molding my fingers

around the lower half of her buttocks and brushing as far between her legs as the fabric will allow.

Then I release her and spin her around. Her face is flushed, pupils dilated. I can't stop myself from claiming her mouth, tasting her sweet lips, giving her just a small sweep of my tongue.

When I break the kiss, she stares up at me, surprise making her blue-green eyes wide.

"Thank you for wearing the skirt, Marissa." My voice sounds three times lower than usual.

I release her completely, not trusting myself not to throw her up on the counter and spread her killer legs. To make her forget about cooking and scream my name until she's hoarse.

But I told her I wasn't paying for sex. And she's on my dime right now.

I wrap my arm behind her and cup her ass, giving it a gentle squeeze. "*Capiche?*"

She rubs her swollen lips together and nods. "Yeah."

"Good girl." One more squeeze. "What's for dinner?"

"Dinner. Um, yeah." She turns to the crate and starts unpacking it. "Almond-crusted salmon with a lemon-thyme sauce, and artichoke salad. You're going to love it."

"Oh, I have no doubt." I lean a hip against the cupboards. I like watching her catch her stride again, moving from discombobulated to self-assured. It takes about ten minutes, but then she settles in, moving around my kitchen like she owns the place. Frying pan on the stove, cutting board and knife out, vegetables diced in neat piles.

"So white wine?" I ask. "Do you want to pick?"

She looks over her shoulder with an expression that gets me harder than marble. It's bright-eyed pleasure. She's all lit up, glowing from doing what she loves, and clearly happy I asked for her opinion. "Yes, what do you have?"

I pull three bottles from the wine chiller and set them on the counter. "You don't get to call the shots at Michelangelo's, do you?"

She scoffs. "Not even what size to chop a vegetable." I love the conspiratorial smile she gives me as examines the bottles. "I dare not vary even the slightest bit from what the chef prescribes."

"That's why you agreed to this."

She selects one of the wines—an oaky Chardonnay—and hands it to me. "Well, yes. It's fun to make my own menu. Especially with someone else's money." Her smug satisfaction transfers to me, filling and warming my chest.

I'm happy to be the guy who made her smug and satisfied. Who gave her the opportunity to show off and the money to spend.

"Speaking of which…" I pull out a wad of cash from my pocket and count out ten hundred-dollar bills. "This is for groceries."

She closes her fingers around the folded bills but doesn't take them from me, meeting my eyes on a swallow. She tries to hide it, but money excites her same as it excites most of the population. "For the month? Or do I just keep a tally and ask for more when this runs out?"

"For this week." I know damn well she didn't spend a thousand bucks on this week's food, but I also want her to be compensated for her time, too. Yes, she owes me. But she also works damn hard, and I imagine this job took up the only spare time she has in her life.

Okay, yeah, I'm a softy.

I'm also showing off.

And I like watching her pretend she's unaffected by it. Her pride is as sexy as those legs.

"Next time you buy the wine, too," I tell her, like I'm being a hardass.

She inhales sharply through her nose and nods. "Gladly."

"But if you don't call me for a ride, the bill's on you."

There. That will get her. I don't know—the wooden spoon might have been too much of an enticement. And I really don't want her denying me the pleasure of keeping her safe.

The threat turns her on. I know because her nipples are visible beneath her bra.

She plays it tough, but she likes it bossy. Maybe because it gives her something to resist.

I uncork and pour two glasses of wine, but apart from tasting it and giving a nod of satisfaction, she doesn't drink any more.

Which shouldn't be such a disappointment, but it is. Maybe I'm reading too much into it, but I think it signals she's not comfortable. She wants to keep her wits around me.

Of course, maybe she just doesn't like white wine. Why not just ask? For fuck's sake, I've turned into the biggest vagina.

"Not a wine drinker?"

She slides a sidelong glance at me. The kind that peeks

under her lashes and looks both sly and demure at once. "I'm on the job."

"True."

I watch her plate the food.

For one.

One plate.

Mine.

"You're staying to eat." I don't make it a question.

To my surprise, tough girl blushes.

Huh.

"The chef doesn't eat with the patrons."

"You're off shift. Make a second plate."

She doesn't move. I don't sense outright resistance. More indecision. "This isn't a date," she clarifies.

"This is you paying off your debt. I want to eat your food, and I want you sitting with me when I try it. Is that too much to ask?"

Cazzo. I'm throwing my weight around like an asshole, but she's not cowed. She twists her lips up in this cute, contemplative way and cocks her head to the side.

"I'll eat with you," she says slowly, "if you'll play the piano for me when we're done."

I manage to get my eyebrows back down in a couple seconds and cock a grin. "What? Don't believe I can play?"

She's already moving, plating the second dinner and grabbing utensils from my drawers. I fucking love the way she makes herself at home and doesn't ask where things are or for help.

"I believe it. I just want to hear it." She carries both plates with utensils rolled up in cloth napkins that she brought over to my table by the window. She sets the table and waits while I pour myself a second glass of wine and bring both glasses to the table to sit. "This is an incredible view."

It is. At night, the lights of the city, as well as the yachts docked along the shore, glitter and reflect off the inky water of Lake Michigan. When I bought this place, I pictured myself showing off the view to women I brought home for one-night stands.

And before the shooting, I did quite a bit of that.

Now, though, I'm not even sure I care about that view. Was it just a symbol of my wealth and power? Or do I actually enjoy looking out at the water?

Fuck if I know.

And that's the problem.

I think I've been living my entire life doing what I thought was fulfilling. Getting my dick wet. Getting rich. Seizing power and throwing my weight around. Violence on occasion to make me feel like a real man.

But none of those things have been enough since I got shot. I don't crave more money. More pussy. Even if Junior hadn't settled the score, I don't think I'd burn for revenge for getting shot. I just can't seem to give three fucks about anything these days.

This little girl in front of me, though. She's something different. And it seems I'm always hard for her.

I lift my wine glass in the air and wait for Marissa's hesitation to pass for her to pick up hers and clink them together. "To our new arrangement."

I see a flicker of anxiety on her face before she nods

firmly. "To our new arrangement." We both drink and I pick up my fork, eager to taste her food.

It's incredible—she used simple ingredients but the tastes explode in my mouth. "*Madonna*, this is good. *Che meraviglia*. It's wonderful."

I love the flushed pleasure on her face. "I made you speak Italian."

I chuckle. "Angel, I'm sure there are quite a few things you could do that would make me break into the old language."

She does that flirty gaze under her lashes again with a smirk.

"*Parli Italiano?*"

She shakes her head with regret. "No. I never learned to speak it. I can understand it okay just from hearing my grandparents talk, but that's it. I want to go there someday. Did you know if you're Italian American you can get Italian citizenship? And college is free to citizens there, so I could go to college in Italy."

"Is that what you want?"

She shrugs and I decide it's not.

"I'll take you there, angel. Show you the Old Country."

A little blush creeps up her neck, and I decide she likes that idea but won't let herself accept it. Just like she couldn't just ask for help with her cousin. She takes a bite of her fish and even though she doesn't make a show of it, I can tell she's satisfied with her creation.

"It's good, no?"

"It turned out."

"Don't be modest. It's delicious." I have to slow my

shoveling down so I don't clear my plate in minutes and make her work seem insignificant.

She's a dainty eater, her soft lips closing delicately around the fork tines in a way that comes off way too sexual for my cock's comfort.

"So how long have you played piano?"

Her interest in the piano is funny to me. It's not a talent I share with anyone but family, so I'm not used to having anyone talk to me about it. "Since I was six. It was Christmas-time and I was at a mall with my ma. Some old black guy with a Santa hat was playing ragtime piano, and I stopped to watch. I'd never heard the sound before, but more than that, I was fascinated with how fast his fingers moved. When he was finished with the song, he invited me over and taught me how to play *Jingle Bells*."

"And then your parents put you in lessons?"

I choke on a snort, then wipe my mouth with a napkin. "Very funny. No, not exactly."

"So, what happened?"

"So, I went home and begged for my own piano. And my dad called me a pansy and told me boys don't play piano. And then I went and punched my brother Paolo."

It's her turn to snort. "Isn't he older?"

"Yeah. I didn't pick on the babies. Punching your older brother is fully allowed, though. Then I could get the beat-down I was craving and have a reason to cry."

The shock on her face tells me I should've stopped at *yeah*.

"Too much. Sorry."

"No, no." She works to hide her dismay. "So, then what happened?"

59

"So, my ma had a fit. She blew up at my dad, and when he wouldn't budge, didn't speak to him for four days. And I got a piano. My dad told me if I didn't practice every fucking day, he'd burn the thing. I practiced every fucking day." I give her a rueful smile.

"You must be good."

I grin. "State champion at age twelve." I scrape the last of her delicious sauce off my plate.

"Do you want more? Was that enough food?"

"I always want more, angel. But I don't need it." I pat my belly.

She rolls her eyes. "I'll make more next time. I don't like fish reheated, so I didn't make extra this time."

I like how she's eager to please. In this aspect, not any other. It turns me on. I pour myself more wine and sit back to watch her eat.

~

Marissa

EVEN THOUGH HE told me state champion, I was unprepared for how incredible Gio plays. His fingers dance over the keys playing an incredible classical song I've heard in movies. Or elevators.

I stand behind him, admiring the ease with which he holds himself, how he looks over at me and winks, like he knows I'm blown away and thinks it's funny.

"What song is this?"

"*Solfeggietto in C.* It sounds more impressive than it is," he tells me. "It's actually just scales."

I laugh incredulously. "No, it's pretty impressive."

But I'm getting itchy. If I stay much longer, Gio's going to think we're having sex. I've already sat down over wine and dinner with him—which I know was probably a mistake. I wish I didn't find him so damn irresistible.

As if Gio picks up on my tension, the moment he finishes the song, he gets up. "I'll drive you home."

"Or just to the train station. I can take the L home."

"The fuck you are."

I roll my eyes, but I knew he was going to say it, and I can't deny the little flame of warmth it ignites. My dark hero. Obsessed with my safety.

I go to the kitchen to clean up.

"Leave them," he orders. "I'll clean up this time."

"*Spaciente*," I say. *Sorry.* "A chef never leaves her kitchen in disorder. It's the cardinal rule."

Gio's eyes are warm on me as he leans in the doorway and just watches me move around. I'm lightning fast— every chef is. There's no place for slow in a kitchen.

"I'd help, but I'm afraid to get in your way," Gio observes.

"You would," I confirm, starting the dishwasher and corking the wine. I wipe down the countertops and wash and dry my hands. "Let's go."

"Seven minutes, twenty-eight seconds," Gio says, looking at his phone. "Impressive."

"I know," I say with a cocky smile. My prowess in the kitchen is one thing I don't worry about.

I gather my things and we head downstairs, Gio taking the handcart and crate from me and pulling it himself. "What's your favorite thing about cooking?" Gio asks in the elevator on the way down.

"My favorite thing?" I almost don't want to tell him. Don't want him to feel like he's doing me a second favor here. But he is. "It's the menu creation. So I enjoy this job."

"This job." he repeats with a nod, like he's reminding himself he's a job to me, not anything more. "Couldn't you do more of that at Milano's?"

I shrug. "Milano's is a cafe. Pastries and coffee. Some deli foods. It's not a gourmet sit-down restaurant."

The elevator doors open and we emerge in the underground parking area. Gio moves closer to me, as if to shield my body with his as we make our way to his SUV.

"Couldn't it be? I'm just thinking— you already have your own place. Why are you working for another chef when you could be doing it for yourself?"

I shake my head. It's not like I haven't dreamed of having my own restaurant. But it would be a nice restaurant. Not some washed up cafe in Cicero. "We don't get the kind of clientele it takes to support the kind of restaurant I'd want."

"What kind is that?"

Jesus, this guy is relentless. And these aren't personal questions, but to me they are. They're at the very essence of all my hopes and dreams. And every one of them bares another bit of my soul.

"Fine dining. Like Michelangelo's."

He loads the handcart in the trunk, then holds the door

open for me. "And you love everything else about Michelangelo's?" he asks when he gets in. "Like you'd rather that were your full-time job?"

I snort. "It is my full-time job. Milano's is my home life. But yeah. Honestly? Sometimes I wish the shooting had..." I stop because it's too wicked to even say out loud.

"Closed the place down?" he finishes.

I exhale and drop my forehead into my fingers. "I shouldn't say that. I'm a terrible granddaughter."

Gio's quiet for a long time, letting me stew in my shame. "I know a shit-ton about being conscripted into a family business," he says gruffly.

I jerk my head up and look over. It never occurred to me that Gio might not enjoy his business. All I see is the power and money. Maybe he has no taste for the violence. Well, crap—he got shot in the gut for it, didn't he? Almost died?

"I'll bet you do," I say softly. I clear my throat. "Anyway, yeah, I'd rather just work at Michelangelo's. Except without my direct boss, because he's disgusting."

I sense Gio's body come alert, even though I didn't say it. I didn't say anything, yet he somehow seems to know. "Disgusting how?" he asks sharply.

Tingles run over my skin. I can't decide if I'm excited or nervous about the threat I hear in his voice. The fact that I know his protectiveness is still aimed firmly at me.

No, this is a problem.

This man is dangerous. Like breaking-legs dangerous. Shooting kneecaps. Busting ribs. I may hate working with Arnie, but I'm not going to send a mafia hitman after him.

Well, I don't know if Gio's a hitman, but he easily could be.

"Never mind." My voice sounds scratchy.

Gio cuts his gaze from the road to me. "What's his name?" His tone is deadly.

I shake my head. "I'm not telling."

Gio's lip curls and he looks downright scary. "The fuck, Marissa?"

My heart's beating fast, like I'm the one in danger and not my asshole handsy boss. "I don't trust you, Gio."

He flinches and the color drains from his face, along with the anger. "Huh," is all he says.

I want to say more—to say it better so he's not offended, although this whole thing is crazy. Since when do I need to be so worried about hurting the feelings of one of the heads of the most powerful crime family in the country?

I don't. I shouldn't. This man pretty much owns me, even though he hasn't flexed that power much, he could. I shouldn't have to worry about him getting butthurt when I don't want him to throw someone in Lake Michigan with cement shoes for me.

Gio

MY FIST SMASHES through the drywall of my bedroom too easily. I squeeze my fingers into a fist, relishing the pain. At least I'm feeling something. First time in months.

Although the self-disgust doesn't exactly answer my question for why the fuck I'm living.

Cristo.

She doesn't trust me. I guess she fucking shouldn't. Because I want to kill that *stronzo* boss of hers. The one who's done something disgusting to her.

And I *know* it's something I'd wanna kill him for, because she wouldn't tell me.

And fuck if my need to fix this for her, to exact a little justice, isn't all-consuming. I smash my fist through the wall again. Two more times.

My knuckles bleed a little.

So she doesn't want me to hurt the guy. That makes me a bad person, I guess.

Cazzo!

In my book, you don't stand around and let a woman get molested by her boss and do nothing. And it's happening to fucking *Marissa,* which makes me violent just thinking about it.

So what the fuck do I do?

What would a good guy do? A real hero?

A fucking hero would kill the *stronzo.*

Wouldn't he?

I don't know. Maybe my world view is just skewed so far toward violence I don't know how to function in this world. Maybe that's why I feel like a whale out of water since my shooting.

And then it occurs to me who does know how to function better within the lines of the law and societal norm.

I glance at the clock. It's 3:00 a.m. Only 1:00 a.m. in Vegas. I pull out my phone and call my younger brother

65

Nico. He owns a casino so he's up late, even with—maybe especially with—a baby at home.

We're not close. Not really. The five Tacone brothers fell into two groupings. The oldest three—me, Junior and Paolo, were one and the younger two—Nico and Stefano were another. We older brothers were expected to take over the family business. Our dad rode us hard and trained us to fit into his mold. Nico and Stefano had a little more leeway.

Which is maybe how they thought out of the box to expand business way beyond what the rest of us ever believed possible. And made it legal in the process.

Nico answers on the first ring. "Gio. What's up?"

I don't speak for a moment, because I don't even know what I want. Whether or not it was a mistake to call.

"Gio?"

"I'm here, yeah. Wanted to run something by you."

"Shoot."

I pause again. "Say you found out a girl's boss was getting handsy with her, but she's a no-go on any violence. Like wouldn't even tell you the guy's name. What would you do?"

"You want revenge or you want to remove her from the situation?"

I inhale. Interesting separation. I had the two glommed together in my brain. "*Cazzo*. I guess I just want her comfortable. I could give up revenge if I knew he wasn't anywhere near her." *Maybe*.

"Easy then. Get him fired. Lean on the owner with cash or threats. If he's the owner, you buy him out. Or get him shut down. Pay someone off to put him out of business. There's a lot of options. Plus, it's not full justice, but you can smile when you think of him unemployed."

"Huh. Why didn't I think of that?"

"Who's the girl?"

"Fuck off."

"That's the thanks I get?"

"*Grazie, fratello.* That's it."

"I got more ideas. For stealthier vengeance—the kind she wouldn't tie to you. Accidents, that kind of thing. If you need that, too."

I crack my swollen knuckles. Do I need that?

Marissa's reaction keeps replaying in my mind. *I don't trust you, Gio.*

I don't fucking like that.

"Nah, I'll try to do it legitimately. Works well for you."

"It does. A little bit of ruthlessness in legit business brings you right to the top. Who's the girl?"

"*Sta 'zitto.*" Shut up.

"Do I know her?"

"Yeah. It's not a thing. I don't know. Just a girl I want to protect."

"You're a good man, Gio."

Am I? I seriously doubt it. Not when I couldn't even come up with one idea that didn't involve violence.

"I'm not. Give Nico Junior a kiss from me."

"Will do. *Buona notte.*"

I end the call, grateful for what Nico reminded me of. I have more than my fists or guns. I have money. And that's just as powerful—maybe more—than my ability to intimidate.

Tomorrow I'll figure out how to buy Michelangelo's,

and I'll fire every fucker Marissa wants me to. New life starts flickering in my cells. Something long dead in me— dead way before the shooting—awakens.

Gio Tacone, a restaurant owner. It's damn close to the dreams I had for my adult life when I was a kid. Before my dad forever quashed them.

I used to picture myself owning a swanky 50s style lounge. The kind Sinatra would sing in, if he were still alive. I guess it would be a piano bar. Someplace I could reign, the Family man could convene, drink and do business, and my baby grand would gleam in the corner, ready for me to wander over, sit down and entertain. I guess I thought it would be the perfect melding of *La Cosa Nostra* and my love for piano. Like I could somehow put the two together in a positive way.

But of course, any career involving the piano—even a swanky Italian piano bar—was violently rejected by my father.

The more I picture it, the more it comes to life. Like what Nico's built for himself only on a small, intimate scale. A swanky place of my own. Fine dining with a menu prepared by the new upstart talent Marissa Milano. A gleaming black baby grand back by the bar.

Hell, yeah.

This could definitely work.

CHAPTER 5

M *arissa*

WE'VE BARELY STARTED our shift—the restaurant's not even open yet, when Michael, Michelangelo's owner/manager, sticks his head in the kitchen and says he needs us all out in the restaurant for a meeting. He seems nervous. A little sweaty, definitely on edge.

My stomach clenches. Is someone getting fired? But why would they need all of us for that? Crap. Is this where he tells us they're going bankrupt? Or that someone's been stealing? It isn't good, whatever it is.

I follow the rest of the kitchen staff out, and that's when my world flips onto its head.

Gio's sitting there, looking devastatingly dapper in his sleek Italian suit and shiny shoes. He's sitting there—not like a customer, but like he belongs. Like he owns the place.

My sense of dread ratchets up.

"I want to introduce you to the new owner of Michelangelo's." Michael flits a nervous hand in Gio's direction. "This is Mr. Tacone, your new boss. He'll be calling the shots around here from now on. I will stay on as manager and consultant for a period of six months."

The twisting in my stomach grows tighter.

Goddamn Gio.

What in the hell does he think he's doing?

He bought the restaurant where I work? For what purpose? To more fully own me? To make sure I answer to him in all areas of my life?

I blink back hot furious tears.

The *nerve.*

Michelangelo's will become the new mafia hangout. Just like Milano's has been for the last forty years. My grandfather finally got out from under the Tacones, and I did my best to preserve that freedom with the new bargain we struck, but Gio made sure I landed right back in the same position. Just like my grandfather, I'm now locked into running a business for the mafia. Probably for the rest of my life, if this works the same as my grandfather's deal did. I won't ever be able to leave. Won't ever be able to move to a different restaurant or start my own.

I just got locked into the exact scenario I had hoped to avoid.

And damn Gio Tacone for looking so devastatingly debonair right now as he steals my future. His lips curve up and he acknowledges us all with a regal inclination of his head.

Asshole.

Seriously. What an asshole.

We head back into the kitchen, and Lilah whispers to me, "Do you think he's related to the Tacone crime family?"

"I can guarantee it."

She must hear the condemnation in my tone because she shoots a look over her shoulder at me as we work beside each other. "Wait… do you know him?"

I lift my shoulders in a sullen shrug. "I'm from Cicero. His family owned my neighborhood growing up."

Lilah whistles. "Holy shit. Do you *personally* know him? I mean, he doesn't know you, right?" There's excitement in her tone, like this is the best gossip she's heard all year.

"Oh, he knows me all right."

"Marissa" —Lilah grabs my arm and stops me from emptying pasta into the pot of boiling water— "what aren't you saying?"

I just shake my head. "Let's just say it's no coincidence he bought this particular restaurant."

Lilah's eyes widen and she cranes her neck to see my face. "Giiiiirl! Are you telling me Mr. Dark and Dangerous is after you? Like wants to be your boss in a *big daddy* kind of way?"

I just shake my head and turn back to what I'm doing. "I can't even… *I can't.*" I'm too upset to let her cajole me into laughter about it. It's not funny.

Gio Tacone went way too far this time.

71

Gio

I ENJOY the fuck out of sitting in the corner of Michelange-lo's and watching the business run. The waitstaff scurries around, throwing me nervous glances, probably feeling the burn of my gaze. They're good at their jobs, though. I won't come in and make a lot of changes. Not without observing how things run for the six months I have Michael on contract.

He didn't want to give up his restaurant, especially with a no-compete clause so he can't open a new one, but I made him a good offer and applied a tiny bit of pressure for good measure. Like mentioning everything I knew about his family. How his mother could use more help in Florida. And his daughter's college bills were probably high.

He got the picture. I wanted him out. I had the cash to buy him out. And I'd appreciate his cooperation. No actual threats were made, although I think my name and reputation are often threat enough in this town.

And buying this place feels like opening a door. Like it could be the thing that was missing from my life—a purpose to throw myself into. Something I will enjoy the fuck out of creating. A place to stave off the stabbing lone-liness. To become a part of something.

To play the fucking piano for people whose last name isn't Tacone.

And yes… as a gift to Marissa. To keep her somewhere I can protect her and let her do what she loves.

I swear to *Cristo,* the shooting changed the fuck out of

me, because I don't even want anything in return. She doesn't have to fuck me. She doesn't have to be my girl.

I have the capacity to make her happy, and it pleases the hell out of me to do it.

I stay the entire night, sampling various dishes, calling for a few drinks. Watching.

And when the restaurant closes up, I tell Michael, "I'll lock up."

He's too befuddled by his new role to argue. He hands me the keys and writes down the security code so I can arm the system. I make a mental note to get the code and keys changed by tomorrow night.

Then I saunter back into the kitchen to watch the clean-up.

Marissa looks exhausted, a line between her brows as if she's been worrying on something. She also ignores me, pretending we don't know each other.

Okay, maybe she doesn't want it to look like she's sleeping with the boss. Which she's not.

Yet.

"Nice work, everyone. All the food I sampled was delicious," I say and most of the kitchen staff shoot me half-wary, half-resentful glances. Well, nobody likes change.

I stand and watch them finish, which has the effect of making everyone scurry around quickly, and start to leave.

Marissa gets the hint and hangs back until they're gone, exchanging a silent glance full of hidden meaning with the other girl who works there when her friend leaves.

"Come on." I tip my head toward the restaurant area. "I'll pour you a drink."

She follows me to the end of the bar. I pour a glass of

the expensive chianti I sampled earlier, but she sets it on the bar and *knees me in the balls*.

"*The fuck?*" I double over. What. The Fuck? Pain shoots all the way up to my stomach, reverberating where I got shot.

"I guess you own me completely now, don't you?" Marissa snaps.

I straighten from when I doubled over. *What?*

"You agreed not to take Milano's only to buy this place? Really, Gio?" She tries to slap my face.

I catch her wrists before the slap lands and slam her back against the wall.

She gasps.

"Careful, angel," I growl through gritted teeth. I still can't even see straight from the agony in my balls and the pain makes me aggressive.

Very aggressive.

I lean my face down into the crook of her neck. "I like to play rough. Keep it up, you're gonna get fucked hard against this wall."

She twists and bites my jaw.

Cristo, was that her answer? She wants me to fuck her? Or is she just fighting back?

And why the fuck do I question my every move with this girl? Clearly it's always gonna be wrong.

I shove the aching bulge of my cock between her legs.

"Here's how it's gonna go," I snarl. My forehead comes down to hers and we glare right into each other's eyes. "Either you apologize real nice for the ball-bust or I'm gonna punish you with this cock until you can't walk straight. *Capiche*?"

I wait.

She pants, glaring back at me.

No apology.

I give it one more beat. Then I switch her wrists to one hand and palm her mound with the other. I'm rough.

No feather-stroking. No light clit-rub.

It's more like a possessive grab.

She's pissed because she believes I want to own her?

I'll fucking own her.

I pull up with my grip, lifting her to her toes.

She bites again—this time my neck. I chuckle darkly. "Bad girl." I rub between her legs, then shove my hand down her pants to get her at her pussy.

She's wet.

The last of my conscience slips away with that discovery.

"Baby, you're about to find out what it means to be owned." I screw a finger inside her and her wild eyes widen. I get a second finger in and thrust up.

She bites down on her lip so hard it bleeds. The little grunt she makes gets my dick rock hard. I fingerfuck her, trying to find her G-spot on the front wall. Eventually I find it—the place where the tissues stiffen up under my touch.

Marissa makes an unintelligible noise.

I'm trying to figure out how to get my dick out while still fingering her and pinning her to the wall. Not gonna work. Too bad it's impossible. I pull my fingers out of her and suck her juices off.

"You want to know what it's like to be owned by Gio Tacone?" I pull her off the wall and twist her wrists behind her back, then push her over one of the dining tables.

I yank my belt out of the loops and she gets scared, looking over her shoulder at me as she tries to straighten.

I push her back down and smack her ass once with the belt. "I wasn't going to whip you, angel, but I will if you need that."

She goes still, listening, breathing hard.

I wind my belt around her wrists and cinch it tight. Then I yank off her pants and panties. She helps me by kicking off her shoes.

Another small sign of consent.

Marissa wants a good hate fuck right now. Craves it as badly as I do.

There's a red mark from the belt blooming on her ass. I like the way it looks, so I spank her some more with my hand.

It feels fucking amazing.

Her little mewls make my aching balls throb more. My palm stings with the impact. I watch her skin turn a pretty blush. Now that I'm going, I don't really want to stop. I could spank her all night.

"You think I bought this place to own you, Marissa? That's what you really think?"

Her ass dances under my slaps and she shifts from foot to foot. "Why else would you?" she shouts back at me.

I spank her even harder, going for the backs of the thighs. She squeals with genuine alarm, and I lighten up and go back to her ass. "I'll tell you why I bought it, angel. Because you didn't want me to rough up your boss, and I needed you to be safe. I bought it so I could fire his ass and give you some more creative freedom."

Marissa makes a strangled sound. She goes perfectly still for a moment, panting hard. Then she tugs harder at her wrists. "Gio," she cries.

"Hush." It's a sharp command. I don't want to hear whatever it is she's going to say. I stop the spanking and pull out my cock. "You know, it's much easier this way, really." I fish a condom out of my wallet and roll it on. "Both of us just agreeing I own you. I was trying too hard to be the good guy." I grip her hips with one hand and my cock with the other and push in. She's so fucking *tight*. "But Tacones aren't good guys. Right, Marissa?"

She whimpers and shifts her hips back to take me deeper.

I brace her shoulder with one hand and hold her hips with the other and drill into her. "You made a role for me. Why not just fucking play it?" It feels so good to be inside her. Her tight wet heat squeezes my cock like a glove, and every time my balls hit her clit, the residual ache from her assault makes me want to fuck her even harder.

"I have a role you can play, too, angel. It's real easy."

Marissa

OH GOD. I fucked things up again. Badly.

Maybe even worse than when I tried to blackmail him,

because back then he was still trying to show me he wasn't what I thought.

But he's right.

I didn't believe he could be anything but what his father was.

And now he's out of patience with me.

I have a pissed off, aggressive mobster, or maybe ex-mobster, fucking my brains out.

I'm not scared, though. He hasn't hurt me. Even after I hurt him.

It's funny how my body instinctively goes into submission under his command. I surrender and open to him. Receive his anger with each violent thrust.

"Gio." I don't know what to say to fix this. Whether it's even fixable, or if he really has gone to the dark side now.

"Keep quiet or I'll stuff my cock in your mouth instead," Gio growls.

He doesn't want my apology. He knows that's what I was about to offer.

Fine. He wants to be pissed off and take it out through rough sex, I'm down.

Honestly, I was down from the beginning, and he knew it. I was just fooling myself when I told him I wasn't having sex with him.

Maybe it was inevitable. From the moment I showed up in his office with my high heels and low-cut blouse, the die was cast. I was offering myself up to the devil. *Take me to hell with you. Make me your queen.*

Gio slides one hand around my throat and uses it to lift

me up, bow my back like an exotic musical instrument, while he continues to fuck me hard.

He doesn't want an apology. What does he want?

What would make this better?

I blurt the first thing that comes to mind. "Own me." My voice sounds teary. Am I crying? "Own me, then, Gio."

I don't even know what I mean by it—am I really consenting to his use of my body? Whatever it means, it was the right thing to say.

Gio bucks harder. His breathing becomes rough and then he comes with a roar that echoes off the restaurant walls.

To my surprise, I come, too. Quick squeezes of my pussy around his cock relieve the need that was burning me up. I'm not an expert when it comes to sex. I had one long-term partner—a boyfriend I lived with for ten months when I was in culinary school. We had sex and I thought it was good, but nothing is like this orgasm.

The squeezing keeps going, pulsing. Every time he eases back and pushes in again, aftershocks bring on another spasm.

I get lost in the sensation of being filled by him.

Satisfied by him.

Used by him.

He pulls out. "Don't fucking move, little girl," he growls.

I don't. I guess I'm eager to please now. Now that I found out this man bought Michelangelo's just to fire Arnie. And to make me happy.

If I can believe him.

Which I think I can.

There's no denying how offended he is right now.

Of course, that could be from the knee to the balls.

I *can't* believe I did that.

The fact that I did tells me I actually know he's not what I've painted him to be.

Would I have kneed Don Tacone in the balls?

Not ever. Not in a million years. The man is murder and danger and power wrapped up into one. Was. He's in jail now.

I wouldn't even dare such a thing with Junior Tacone. Or any of the other brothers. No. I did it because I actually know Gio's safe.

He returns and unwinds the belt from my wrists and tosses my purse beside my head. "If you need to let someone know you won't be home, do it now."

My breath leaves my chest with a whoosh. He really is making a claim on me.

The result is more excitement than anything. This tough, angry side of Gio curls my toes. Melts my panties.

There's something about a take-charge guy, especially when it comes to sex, that turns me to mush. And having it in Gio's handsome, normally charming package makes it all the more enticing.

My fingers shake as I pull my phone out and text Aunt Lori that I'm going home with a co-worker.

"Done." I say, daring to meet his eye for the first time since he had me pinned against the wall. I'm still naked from the waist down, but that's nothing compared to how vulnerable it feels just to look at him.

"I'm s—"

He covers my mouth with his hand. "Save it, angel. The time for sorry is past. We've moved on to ownership, and I'm rather enjoying it." He stoops to pick up my panties and hands them to me, then shakes out my pants.

"I need a shower," I blurt, suddenly embarrassed of my state. If he's taking me home for more… *whatever,* I definitely need to get cleaned up. I just worked eight hours in a kitchen—I must smell like food and sweat. And my hair is all flat from my chef's hat.

"That can be arranged." He's still acting gruff with me.

I slip on the pants and pick up my purse. Funny how when he turns tough, I go docile. My, how the power dynamic has shifted. He let me throw my weight around before. Call a few shots.

Tell him no.

Now he's boss, and I'm the bad girl.

Although deep down I still believe I could tell him no. He gave me a choice when he had me pinned up against that wall.

Even mad, he was careful with me.

I wait while he locks up and we head out. I'm holding my jacket instead of wearing it, and I shiver against the chill. Gio immediately takes it from my arms and holds it out, helping me shrug it on.

He may have claimed ownership of me, but he's still a gentleman. I'm soothed by the simple act.

Whatever Gio has in store for me, I'll be safe. I'm sure of that.

CHAPTER 6

 io

I STRETCH out on my back on my bed in my boxer briefs and listen to the sound of the shower running in the master bath.

I'm an asshole. Maybe I've always been an asshole pretending to be a decent man.

Maybe I just never thought about it much before.

I'm still pissed over how Marissa sees me, which is stupid. Who's to say I'm not that man? I'm a Tacone.

I can take what I fucking want.

I don't have to ask permission first.

Marissa Milano is gonna learn that tonight.

The thing that's killing me is that it would still be so easy for me to let her off the hook. Accept her apology and send her home with cab fare. But she wants this.

Own me, then, Gio. I'll never fucking forget the throaty sound of that cry. Or the way it felt to fully claim her.

I'd never tell anyone, but she's the first woman I've had sex with since I got shot. First I was afraid my dick wouldn't cooperate—I still had so much pain and didn't feel like myself.

Then I just lost interest in women as I lost interest in life. But Marissa sure as hell showed me everything's working fine.

A-okay down there.

In fact, ready for round two.

I pull my cock out of my briefs and give it a hard yank.

The shower turns off. My cock surges with anticipation.

And then my fucking conscience pricks again. Maybe it's because she's so much younger than I am. Or because of the nightmares and my irrational need to protect her from the danger that haunts her in them.

Or fuck, because I could die tomorrow and don't want to feel I ever took a girl against her will.

But then Marissa opens the door and stands there, completely, gloriously naked. And she takes one look at me with my dick in my hand and comes straight to me.

Fuck you, conscience. You worry-for-nothing-pig-whore.

Marissa crawls over me, straddling my thighs and reaching for my cock.

I'm never the passive one in bed, but I let her drive. It's fucking hot to see that she wants to give me this. My cock lengthens and thickens in her palm and she doesn't tease. She takes me deep on the first bob.

I jack my hips up, shoving into the back of her throat without meaning to.

She chokes but doesn't pop off. She sucks hard, her tongue swirling on the underside of my stiff member.

"*Cazzo*, angel." My hand tangles in her wet hair.

She's fucking beautiful. Perfect because she's Marissa. Small tits. Little roundness to her belly, long slender legs.

I use my hand in her hair to push her forward and back over my cock, careful not to choke her again. She hums.

The girl's giving me a fucking hummer.

I adjust my grip, pulling all her hair back from her face and twisting it around my fist. "Aw, you are a sorry girl, aren't you, angel?"

"Mmm." She keeps up the humming. It's so fucking hot and sweet. I love it. I want it to go on forever, but my balls are already drawing up tight.

I pull her off. "As much as I'd love to see you swallow, angel, I have other plans for you tonight."

She sits up, a little sex nymph, her pert breasts pointing at me, her expression so fucking willing.

Own me, then, Gio.

She asked for this.

"Over my lap, angel. I'm going to spank that ass again before I fuck it." I sit up with my back against the headboard and tug her over my thighs. "I fucking loved spanking this ass earlier," I say, stroking my palm over her soft skin. "Did you like it, doll?"

She doesn't answer.

I deliver a swat. "Hmm?"

She turns her face toward me. "It seems like a dangerous thing to admit."

I chuckle because I knew I was right—she loved it. "Aw, you can trust me, angel. I'm not going to hurt you."

I love her little smile. She rolls her hips, which I take as an invitation to spank her some more, and I do, turning her skin a lovely shade of pink. Then I slide my fingers between her legs, rubbing her sweet nectar up to her clit. "Might have to spank you every time, angel. Do you feel how wet you are?"

She shivers as I slide two fingers inside her and pump them a few times. "Spread your thighs, baby."

She opens wider for me. I stroke over her slick flesh, getting her clit stiff and hot. I use some of her lubricant and bring my index finger to her anus, massaging it open.

She whimpers and tries to tighten, but my finger's already in. I drop a little saliva on top of it to help lube the way. "Have you taken it in the ass before, little girl?"

"N-no." She sounds a little scared now, but I don't mind. I know what I'm doing and she's gonna like it.

"Well, you're gonna take it in the ass for me, baby. Any time I want you to. *Capiche*?"

Cristo, she's rubbing her nipples over the bedspread. "You're mean," she pants as I ass-fuck her with my finger.

"I own you, baby, remember? You said it first."

"I know. Gio, I'm sorry."

"I know you are, baby." It's easy to accept an apology when she surrendered so fully. I ease my finger out of her anus and slap her ass again. "Lie on your belly. Pillow under your hips to lift your ass for me." One more smack.

She complies as I get up and retrieve a bottle of lube from my nightstand drawer. I'm generous with it—squirting some over her anus as well as all over my cock.

I straddle her thighs and push her cheeks wide. "Deep breath in," I command.

She inhales. I push the head of my cock against her back pucker and apply a little pressure. "Exhale."

As she does, I gently push in. It's a stretch to get past the head, but I go slowly.

She grunts, tiny little moans.

"Big exhale again, angel." I ease the rest of the way in and wait for her to get used to me. "If you want to slide your fingers between your legs and play with that sweet pussy of yours, you can."

She immediately moves, like it's a desperate need.

I brace my weight on my hands and rock into her ass. I like the power of having her under me, submitting to this erotic punishment. I like the tight squeeze, the taboo of the thing.

I *fucking love* the sound of her little gasps and mewls as I pick up speed. I love it even more when she starts moaning my name. "Gio... Gio."

"That's right, angel. Who owns you?"

"You do. Oh my God, you do. Holy hell, Gio." I hear her fingers working frantically between her legs.

I fuck her harder, faster, careful not to be too rough or erratic with my strokes. My balls tighten, heat flares at the base of my spine. I pull out and pump my cock, coming all over her ass.

She cries out, her hips lifting from the pillow as she brings her other hand between her legs. As soon as I'm done coming, I shove three fingers and my thumb in her pussy from behind, making a cone to fuck her with until she screams and comes all over my fingers.

~

Marissa

GIO GETS up and returns with a washcloth, which he uses to clean me. Then he brings me a glass of water. "You okay, angel?"

I nod and drink deeply before handing him the glass back. He's in all his naked, manly glory. Broad, buff shoulders, hairy chest, thighs like tree trunks. His five o'clock shadow gives him a rugged look.

"Climb under the covers, I'm gonna take a quick shower."

"'Kay." I'm feeling very much like a bad girl. A little ashamed. A little punished. A lot used. Definitely owned.

My anus pulses, raw and sore from the activity, but the rest of my body is replete with relaxation and the feel-good hormones that go with two orgasms in one night.

I crawl under the covers, surprised when Gio waits to pull them up and kiss my temple. The sweetness of it makes my heart pick up speed. I had been sleepy, but now my mind churns, turning over and examining everything that happened tonight.

He takes care of me.

I haven't had that before. Not ever. My mom abandoned me with my grandparents when I was six and they were kind to me, of course, but they were already old and overworked. They needed my help. No one had time to baby me.

I think of all Gio's done for me. There's the money,

which is sort of his line of work, so that doesn't count. But driving me to the hospital to pay for the surgery. Waiting outside Michelangelo's to drive me home.

Buying Michelangelo's to fire my boss.

I still can't believe that one.

Gio emerges from the shower, a towel wrapped around his waist. I turn over in the bed when he drops it and climbs in.

"Is it true? You really bought Michelangelo's to fire my boss?"

Gio leans up on his forearm. "I swear to Christ. You can call my brother, Nico and he'll tell you. It was his idea."

I blink at him, suddenly fascinated by everything about Gio Tacone—his brothers, his history, his motivations. "Which one is Nico?"

"He's a younger brother. He lives in Vegas."

"He runs your casino"

"Well, it's his casino, but I'm a stakeholder, yeah."

"So, what? You called him? About me?" I'm feeling bold, I guess, because I stretch my fingertips out to scrape them through his chest hair.

One corner of his mouth ticks up and he brushes my outstretched arm with his thumb. "Yeah. You didn't want me to kill the guy. Nico's proven himself to be good at— you know—more *legal* solutions to problems."

Now I smile. I sort of love these glimpses into the real Gio. Not the slick charmer, but the straight-talker.

"And he told you to buy the restaurant?"

"Yeah. Or apply pressure to the owner, but I didn't

think you'd like that, either. I'm trying to be good, here, Marissa. But it keeps biting me in the ass with you."

My heart's pounding now.

He's trying to be good… *for me?*

How is it possible I attracted the attention of such a powerful man? And moreover, that he's worried about doing things right for me?

I scoot a little closer on the bed. "I'm sorry again for misconstruing your actions."

He moves slowly—maybe slow enough I could stop him if I wanted—and reaches for my head. He cradles his large hand around the back of it and pulls my face up to his.

One kiss.

More like a taste. He slides his lips over mine and lets me go.

"You taste good."

"So do you," I whisper.

He tweaks one of my nipples. "So you gonna tell me which asshole I'm gonna fire?"

I let out a laugh with a breath. "Arnie. He's so gross. And I'm not the only one he tries things with—he's molested Lilah, too."

"The other line cook?"

"Yeah, she's awesome. You should give her a raise."

Gio's mouth twists into a smile. "Noted." He brushes a strand of my hair out of my eyes. "You want the head chef position?"

"Me? Are you nuts? No!"

"Why not?"

"I'm not experienced enough. I mean, I've only been a line cook for a year now."

Gio cocks his head at me. "Don't you have a degree from some culinary institute?"

"Well, yeah, but—"

"But what? Don't you want to plan menus and create your own thing, like you did here for me?"

I scrape my fingers through his chest hair again. "I-I'm not ready for that."

"You'll take Arnie's position, then. As sous chef."

"I can't. Really, Gio. Don't do that."

He narrows his eyes. "Why not?"

"Because if people find out we—" I stop, because I don't know what *we* are. "They'll say I fucked my way into the job. Especially if you fire Arnie and put me in it right away. No one will respect me. I want to work my way up. Earn it."

Gio frowns. "We're gonna table this conversation for a later date."

I breathe out a sigh of relief. I can live with that. "Okay. Thank you, Gio." I snuggle in even closer, until we're skin to skin, and press my face against his chest. He smells clean and delicious. He wraps an arm around me and pulls me in tight. Our legs tangle beneath the covers.

"There was another reason I bought Michelangelo's," Gio says.

I go still. Shit. Was I right after all?

At first he doesn't go on, and I'm about to prompt him when he says, "When I was a kid— way back, before I fully understood that my father was never gonna let me play piano in public, I had this idea."

I lift my head from his chest. "What was it?"

He clears his throat. "I... well, dreamed about owning a piano bar. Some place I could be the host and schmooze with people and maybe wander over and play the piano whenever I felt like it." His gaze is wary, like he thinks I'm about to make fun of him.

It's a crazy moment. Gio Tacone—dangerous, powerful, beautiful man—is showing me this piece of vulnerability.

"Your father was a prick."

"Watch it," he growls, but it seems almost automatic. His gaze still holds oceans of vulnerability.

"He was." I'm suddenly extremely pissed off for Gio. What kind of asshole father squashes his son's dream of playing piano because he thinks it's not masculine enough? What a jerk. "You'll make the perfect restaurant/piano bar host."

"I don't know if a piano would really go at Michelangelo's. I guess fine dining is in silence? I mean, in terms of music?"

I shrug. "So what? It can be silent during dinner and then after the kitchen closes at ten, it could turn into a lounge for the last few hours. I bet you'd pack the place."

"You think?"

"It's perfect, Gio. Really." I don't know why I'm so enthusiastic about changing Michelangelo's into the very Tacone hang-out I was so pissed imagining earlier. I guess I recognize what it is to have a dream. A vision of where you think you'd fit in life. And he has the finances and ability to make his dream come true, unlike most of us. In fact, he has the ability to make my dreams come true, too, not that I'm going to let him.

I already owe the man too much. He's already saying he owns me.

I can't let him own my dreams, too.

Then there'd be nothing of me left to keep.

CHAPTER 7

 io

I STEP INTO CAFFÈ MILANO. I'm looking for Ivan, the bratva *asshole I'm supposed to meet. I find him sitting at a table across from Marissa. At least I think it's Marissa. Her back is to me. Ivan watches me as I approach, a smug smile on his face. I walk over and Marissa looks up. Duct tape is over her mouth, and I see her wrists and ankles are bound together. She tries to scream from behind the tape. Her wide and frightened eyes are glued to mine.*

Glued to mine as Ivan laughs and shoots her right in the heart.

"No!" I shout and reach for my gun, but it's not there. It's not there and someone's pulling my arm.

I try to jerk it off.

"Gio."

95

I blink. Marissa's wide blue gaze is still fixed on my face. "Gio." She tugs on my arm.

"Marissa." Thank fuck. There's no tape over her mouth. She's not bleeding. She's in my bed.

Just a dream. Just a fucking dream.

She traces her fingertips over the muscles of my arm. "Another nightmare?"

"*Cazzo.*" I rub the stubble on my face. "I'm sorry. Did I wake you?"

"Was I in it?"

I give a humorless laugh. "Every fucking time."

"What happened? Never mind." She shakes her head. "I don't know why I asked. I'm sure I don't want to know."

"You definitely don't. Fucking Russians." I throw the covers off and pad to the bathroom. When I come back, Marissa's still in my bed.

I stop to take in the sight.

She's so fucking pretty. Her caramel-colored hair fans out on the pillow, the blue of her eyes bright against the backdrop of my charcoal gray sheet she has pulled up to her armpits. She's so young and fresh and full of life. So much to live for. And it could all be taken away in the blink of an eye.

I climb back onto the bed and yank the sheet down to her waist to see those perky little breasts in the light of the day.

She gasps and tries to reach for it, but I shake my head and she instantly stills, her pretty eyes attentive and alert.

Huh. She's submissive with me now.

Not a submissive by nature, though.

I straddle her waist over the sheet and palm one of her breasts.

All her attention's still trained on my face. I see the flutter of her pulse in her neck. "They're small," she murmurs, like an apology.

I release her tit and slap the side of it.

She yelps and covers both of them with her hands.

"They're fucking perfect." I grab her wrists and pin them down beside her head. "You criticize this body again, I'm gonna paint your ass red."

She lets out a surprised laugh. "It's my body."

I arch a brow. "Is it baby? I don't think so. I believe I own you now." I cup both her breasts and squeeze, then brush my thumbs over the stiffened peaks.

My cock lengthens between us.

She licks her lips.

I slide the sheet down between us and run my finger over her slit to check for wetness.

Dripping.

Babygirl likes being owned.

And I sure as hell love owning her.

I move to the side to get rid of the topsheet and slip my hands behind her knees to push them up toward her shoulders.

"That's right baby. Spread that pussy for me and show me how wet you get when I talk dirty."

She whimpers. I can't get enough of those eyes trained on my face! It makes me feel as tall as the fucking Willis Tower.

"That's the pussy I own, isn't it, baby?"

She sucks her lower lip into her mouth, her breath coming more quickly.

"What should I do to that pussy first? Lick it?"

She swallows and nods quickly.

I give her what must be a feral smile. I'm definitely feeling predatory. I lower my head and take one long lick with my tongue flat. Then I trace around her inner lips.

"You make all that honey for me, angel?"

Whimper.

"Does that mean you want my big cock inside you again, sweet girl?"

"Yes," she says quickly. More quickly than I expected. It's so fucking cute.

So fucking hot.

My balls start aching. I nip her labia and she gasps. Moving her legs to rest on my shoulders, I reach up and take hold of each of her nipples, applying a steadily increasing pressure as I tickle her clit with my tongue.

"Oh my gawd!" she cries.

"You like that, baby?"

"More," she whimpers.

"Oh, I'll give you more. I'll give you so fucking much you'll be begging for mercy."

She mewls because I'm pinching her nipples pretty hard. I speed up the action on her clit, then suction my mouth over it and suck. I release her from both sensations all at once, and she cries out with alarm.

"I need a condom," I tell her. "You put yourself in the position you want to get fucked in. And make it a good one."

As if there's any that wouldn't be good with this girl—ha.

I walk to the nightstand, pretending not to watch as she rustles around on the bed, arranging and rearranging herself. I waste a little time until she goes quiet then let myself take her in.

Fuuuuuuck.

The little minx is on her knees and forearms, ass in the air.

"Oh, babygirl, that was such a good choice. I'm gonna have to reward you for that one."

I walk around behind her and give her dripping cunt another generous massage with my tongue.

"I have to say… this ass is begging to be spanked." I slide my hands around the globes of her ass in total and complete appreciation. "Only one mark from last night. That was from the belt, I think." I trace it with my thumb. "Does it hurt?"

"No."

"Good. I'm not gonna hurt you this morning. I'm just going to give you a little sting. You like it as rough as I like to give, don't you, angel?"

She doesn't answer.

I slap her ass. "Answer me, Marissa."

"I don't know… I guess so."

"Did you learn something new with me?" I rub the place I slapped.

"Yeah. Definitely."

I chuckle, loving her admission. "Beautiful girl." I slap the same place, rub again. I keep going, delivering slaps, then massaging until her skin turns pink and she's moaning and wagging her hips for more.

Only then do I roll on my condom. "Ready for more, angel?"

"Yes, please," she moans.

So sweet she's become. I'm not fool enough to think this will last, but I sure as hell am enjoying it for the moment.

I prod her entrance gently, then ease in. Her moan is sultry. Welcoming. "Such a beautiful ass, baby. I love fucking you from behind."

"Mmm."

I grip her waist and pull her hips back to meet me on my thrusts. The angle lets me get deep inside her and she feels so good. Still tight as a glove. So hot and wet. I close my eyes and indulge in the decadence of sensations.

Finally, a reason to live.

When her cries change in pitch—getting louder and more desperate, I reach around the front of her and rub her clit.

She shrieks. "Gio! Oh my God! Please!"

Who can deny her? I fuck harder, rocking the bed against the wall with the force of my thrusts.

When I'm about to come, I reach around again for another rub. I shout. She screams. We both fly over the edge together, her pussy squeezing my cock in the most glorious way. I fall on top of her and drag her to her side, still buried deep.

I breathe into her neck. Bite it. Hold her breast as I thrust a few more times.

"Oh my God," she pants again.

I trail kisses along her shoulder, down her arm. "All this time I've been wondering why my life was saved," I rumble, not even censoring myself. It's kinda crazy how much I let loose around this girl. "And I think I just figured it out." I nip her arm.

Her laugh is low and throaty. "Oh yeah? For sex?"

"Sex with you, sugar."

I pull out before the condom comes off and I dispose of it.

I pick up my phone and text Michael, who is now essentially my bitch. *Fire the sous chef Arnie, effective immediately. He's been nasty with the girls who work in the kitchen. And give both the girls a three dollar an hour raise, starting from their last paycheck to make it up to them.*

I turn my phone around and show Marissa when I'm done.

She's sitting up in bed, hair tousled, face flushed. She's the sweetest thing I've had in my bed, ever.

I'm trying to figure out how to keep her here. Or if that's even the right thing to do.

Fuck me with this right and wrong shit all the time now. Why'd I have to grow a fucking conscience after my near-death experience?

Marissa

I GRAB Gio's phone to make sure I'm reading the text

101

correctly. A smile forms on my lips as I re-read. "You gave me a raise, too?" I know I'm letting him hear my excitement. It's stupid. Three dollars an hour is nothing to Gio Tacone, and I didn't want to give him any more leverage on me. But what the hell—he's already decided he owns me. Might as well let him pay for it, right?

It occurs to me I should ask for more.

Especially considering how affectionate he's being with me.

But maybe he's like this with every woman he brings home.

A shard of jealousy pierces through me with unexpected viciousness.

"What?"

Damn, he's observant.

I pull the sheet up to cover my breasts. I need to get myself out of here. I am so out of my depth with this man and this only ends one way—with me crushed beneath his boot.

"Are you finished with me now?"

His brows slam down. "What the fuck just happened?"

I get up and start to crawl off the bed, but he catches me by the waist and tugs me back. "Hang on just a minute. What the fuck did I do, Marissa? You mad about the money?"

I can't meet his eyes. I just want to get out of here. I turn my face away. "No, I just—"

He catches my jaw and holds it firmly, turning my face to his. "What'd I do?"

I want to throw something mean in his face about him

owning me and treating me like a whore, but I know in my heart it's a lie, so I let the real problem slip.

"You're a playboy, Gio. I can't do this." I choke on the emotion that pops up. What the hell is this? Just yesterday I was giving him hell and kneeing him in the balls. Now I'm choking up over not being his one-and-only? It's freaking crazy.

"What?" He's as shocked as I am. "No, no, no, no, no. You're nuts, Marissa. You're the first woman I've slept with since I got shot. And that was months ago." He releases my jaw, his touch becoming gentle as he tips my chin up. "You're the girl in my dreams, angel. Just wish they were nice dreams."

He lowers his forehead to mine, his lips hovering over my mouth.

I take the initiative and kiss him. The moment I do, he launches into action, pushing me to my back on the bed, covering my body with his. His kiss is deep, relentless. His tongue sweeps into my mouth, he sucks my lower lip. He consumes me.

It's the best kiss of my life.

A *real* kiss.

Better than any movie.

Better than sex, even.

Well, maybe not better than sex with Gio. That's pretty untoppable.

When he breaks it, he stares down at me. "What do you want from me, angel? I'll give it to you. It's just fucking hard when you won't ever take it."

And then I'm crying.

Hot tears that drip from the corners of my eyes down

my temples. "I'm sorry." I loop my arms around him and pull him close, into a full body horizontal hug. He's heavy, but the weight soothes me. "This is all scary and new to me."

"What is?" He sounds demanding and I think he realizes it, because he repeats the words, more softly, "What is, angel?"

"Everything. You. Who you are. What you represent. The power, the money. The sex."

"Whoa, whoa, whoa. You lost me, baby." He tries to push away to see my face, but I keep a stranglehold on his neck. I really can't take the eye contact right now. "What are you talking about?"

I don't want to say, "you're mafia" because I think it's something you don't say to these guys, so I say, "You're a Tacone."

His weight slumps against me, like I just shot him down. "Baby, I don't even know who I am anymore." His voice is heavy. He sounds ancient. "Ever since I got shot, I don't know what the point of this life is. I meant it when I said you gave me new meaning. So if you have some idea about who the fuck I am, could you please just... forget it? Can we just start from today? This minute. Just two people who like the way their bodies fit together? Who like the way they feel when they're with the other?"

I catch my breath. Whoa. Is that how he feels about me?

He pushes back and this time I reluctantly let him see me. "Do I make you feel good, angel?"

Tingles rush over my skin. He phrased it like it's about

sex, but I can tell by his gaze that he's asking about so much more. Does he?

He scares me. I've been afraid of getting involved with him. But yeah. He definitely makes me feel good. Not just my body.

Me.

I remember how strong I felt going into the hospital with him. How sexy and confident I felt cooking for him.

How freaking special I feel every time he shares something like this about his real struggles. About who he really is.

"Yes, Gio," I whisper. "I like the way you make me feel."

The corners of his mouth lift. "Good. Now, what can I do for you this morning? Take you to breakfast? What time do you have to be at work?"

"Not until two. And I'm making you breakfast." I'm suddenly full of energy, excited to be the version of me he finds so attractive. "Ever have a woman cook for you in the nude?" I ask, traipsing toward the door. "Scratch that, I don't want to know the answer," I call as I sashay toward the kitchen.

"No," he calls after me. "Never, baby. You're the only woman I ever let in my kitchen!"

I'm absurdly pleased with that answer. When you grow up Italian—or at least in my family—you learn that cooking is love. My nonna still spends an entire day preparing a meal for the family dinner. At Christmas, she spends two days making cookies with Mia.

You can taste the love in the food. It's the reason Milano's always has customers.

It's the reason I wanted to become a chef—I wanted to take it to a new level.

I head into the kitchen and tie the apron I left in his drawer around my waist and look through the refrigerator to see what he's eaten of the food I left him.

Gio comes to sit at the breakfast bar in a t-shirt that stretches to accommodate his barrel chest and a pair of running shorts. He rubs his jaw and growls when he takes in my outfit. "Baby, you cook for me like that, you're the only thing that's gonna be eaten."

I smile smugly and ignore him, going about my work.

I'm pleased to find he's devoured almost everything I left. I cut up a little of the steak that should be for tonight's meal and chop some tomatoes, onions, garlic and basil. Then I pull out eggs, butter and milk and make two big fat omelets.

"I can't find it in me to feel guilty you're in my kitchen before you have to go in and cook all night," Gio says when I slide a plate in front of him. He picks it up. "Bring yours over to the table. And you're sitting on my lap. You think I can touch this food before I touch you?"

I think I'm blushing. I want to keep my resistance up to his charm, but he keeps chipping away at my defenses. I carry my plate to the table and gasp at the view. I saw it at night, but in the daytime, it's even more spectacular. Sun streams in through the wall-to-wall windows, sparkles on the waves of Lake Michigan below us.

"This is incredible."

He pulls me down on his lap, as promised. His lips immediately find my breast and he sucks my nipple until I squirm on his lap, the corresponding tug between my legs growing stronger.

"Beautiful girl. I'm starving but you're the only thing I want to eat."

"Don't offend me—I made this food for you. *Mangia, mangia*, as my nonna would say."

"Mmm, all right," he says reluctantly and helps me stand. "Food first." He slaps my bare ass as I turn to take a seat opposite him.

We're silent as we eat. I split my gaze between the view and his handsome face as he shovels the food into his mouth, bobbing his head and making appreciative sounds.

"You were always my favorite Tacone brother," I admit, wiping my lips with a cloth napkin.

He studies me, amused. "Didn't know you thought about any of us enough to even have a favorite."

"Oh I thought about you plenty," I admit. "You were always kind. You and Stefano. The rest of your brothers scared me."

"Yeah. We're the faces," he says. When he can see I don't understand, he elaborates, "The ones who do the schmoozing, when it has to be done."

It brings back home what he is. Who he is. A crime lord. A killer. A member of one of the most dangerous and powerful mafia families in the country. My stomach tightens.

What in the hell am I doing here? This isn't a game and I'm in way over my head.

I pick up our plates but Gio takes them from me. "I'll clean up, doll. Thanks for breakfast."

"I'm going to take a shower and go. I need to get home to change before work."

"I will drive you," Gio says firmly.

"No, I'm good. It's broad daylight. Really."

Gio stops in the entryway to the kitchen and frowns. He looks at me like he's going to say something, then just shakes his head and turns into the kitchen.

I take it as a reprieve and escape to his luxurious bathroom. I need to get away from this crazy fantasy world and back to who I am. The Milano girl. Granddaughter of Luigi Milano, who should've known better than to get herself tangled in Tacone business.

CHAPTER 8

io

I SHOULDN'T HAVE LET her run.

Or maybe it was the right thing to do. I don't fucking know.

I feel like I need to see a shrink, like fucking Tony Soprano or something.

Why is it with Marissa Milano things just get muddier and muddier? That's not true. They get crystal clear and then they fall apart.

There were moments when she was at my place, when I felt like a new man. When I found the me who's been buried under the mold of the Family man. The person I really am. The man I was meant to be.

There were glimmers of purpose and hope. Of possibilities I never believed possible. More like a feeling or energy than a real concrete vision of a future.

But the resonance of it was incredible.

It's still sustaining me, even though the darkness creeps back in more and more every day.

She needed space. I could tell by the way she scampered out of here, refusing to let me drive her home. Refusing to accept any more favors from me.

So I stayed away for the last week. I haven't been into Michelangelo's or Milano's while she's been working. I haven't texted or called.

But tonight's her night to come and cook for me, and I'm really fucking looking forward to it.

Still, there's a point when you gotta stop chasing. I've said before, I'm not the kinda guy who has to pay women. I don't need to force or coerce. So if this one doesn't want me, I'm not gonna press the issue.

That's what I decided.

It's reinforced when the doorman calls up to say she's downstairs. She didn't call me for a ride.

If she shows up in a skirt and heels, eager to please, then I'll know where I stand.

I get up to unlock and crack the door, but then I go back to my computer at the dining room table.

She taps on the door and pushes it open.

Jeans and a fucking t-shirt.

Okay. That's a clear message.

So I'll leave her the fuck alone.

I just call my greeting from where I'm sitting. Like she's the help. And I'm the boss.

Which is actually the case and how I need to leave things.

She gets busy making the food while I look through Michelangelo's financials. Except I don't know what the fuck I'm looking for. I used a broker to buy the business. He established the value, and I doubled it to make my offer irresistible.

But I know jack about running a restaurant except how to eat in one. I forward the info off to Nico with the note:

Took your advice, brother. I'm now the proud owner of Michelangelo's. Would you mind taking a look at the financials and letting me know what you think?

Marissa comes in with a plate of beautiful food. Pork chop with some kind of dried currant and berry sauce and steamed asparagus that is exactly the right tenderness and buttery goodness.

I resist the urge to make her sit with me. Resist the urge to touch her.

When she comes to clear my plate, though, she stops and swallows. "You mad at me?"

Oh, sugar. Now I can't stop myself. My hand reaches for her waist, slides to the back of her jeans where I squeeze her ass. "You trying to make me mad?"

She sucks in a breath her pupils dilating. "No. I mean, I wasn't, but…"

"You need me to turn this ass red again?" I squeeze another handful because it feels so. Damn. Good.

She leans into me.

Fuck.

So much for keeping my hands off her.

I tug her onto my lap and firmly cup between her legs with one hand. With the other, I grab a fistful of her hair and tug her head back. "Babygirl, here's the score. I'm tired of watching you scamper away like you think I'm gonna bite. So if you want my hands on you, you need to make it clear. Give me a fucking, *yes, please.* Otherwise I'm cutting you loose. Tell me now."

Cristo. Sometimes I shock even myself with what comes out of my mouth with this girl. And the truths she pulls from me are even more surprising.

I definitely shocked her. Her blue eyes are wide, pupils huge. She's squirming against my fingers, panting over the stress on her scalp.

"Yes, please," she whispers.

My chuckle is dark and possessive.

My desire is black as night.

The things I want to do to this girl.

The things I'm going to do.

I tug her knees wide, throwing her legs over the outside of mine and slap her pussy with three sharp smacks. Then I grind the seam of her jeans over her clit.

She wriggles and moans.

"You gonna be my good girl?" My voice is gravel-dirty. Dangerously gruff.

"N-no."

I slap her pussy again.

"Yes!" she yelps. "Yes?"

I bite her ear. "You aren't sure?"

"Wh-what do you want?"

I laugh. "That's right, angel. It *is* about what I want,

isn't it? Because you know I'm gonna make it good no matter what I do. Don't you, baby?"

She cups her own breasts. My dirty talk has thrown her over the edge into full on sexual excitement. I get the feeling it's unknown territory for her, and I fucking love how brave she is.

"Let's get this off for starters." I pull her t-shirt over her head.

She reaches to unbutton her jeans.

I catch her hands. "Uh uh. Did I say remove your pants?"

She stops, confused.

"Maybe I want them on." I can't think of any good reason to keep them on at the moment, but I feel like calling all the shots. I'm so done with pussy-footing around this girl. If she wants my touch, she'd better fucking submit.

"Bra off," I order.

She unhooks it and slides it off her arms. I cup both her breasts and pinch the nipples.

"What did I tell you about these breasts?"

"Um… I don't know."

I slap her pussy, then return to rolling the nipples between my forefingers and thumb. "I said they're perfect. Now you say it."

"Oh, Jesus, Gio."

"Say it, babygirl. You already have a punishment coming."

"For what?"

"You know what for."

She gulps as I rub the seam of her jeans against her clit again. "They're perfect," she mumbles.

"Louder. Say *my tits are fucking perfect*. Loud and proud, baby."

"Oh my God, Gio. You're nuts."

I pinch both nipples tight and hold. Bite her shoulder. "Say it."

"My tits are fucking perfect!" she squeals.

I release her nipples and she mewls.

I push her up to stand. "Bend over the table, baby."

She shoots me a nervous look over her shoulder but turns back to the table and slides her fingertips over the surface until her bare breasts are flattened against the glass.

"Now that's a pretty sight." I stand up and unbuckle my belt. She shoots another nervous glance over her shoulder.

"I'll let you keep your jeans on for your spanking, pretty girl. I wouldn't want to leave marks."

She sinks her teeth into her lower lip and turns back to face the table. I can see her reflection in the glass. She's excited.

"Spread your legs." I nudge her feet wider.

I wrap the buckle end of my belt around my fist and try it out on my leg. I'm just playing— I definitely don't want to hurt Marissa.

Tempering the strokes, I let the belt swing, careful not to let the tail wrap around her hip.

She gasps.

I rub all over her ass, rub between her legs, squeeze. "You okay, baby?"

"Yes, please."

I laugh. "Please, huh? That mean you want more?"

"Um, yes? I think so."

"Tip your ass back and show me you're gonna be a good girl for your spanking."

She does and I deliver five quick stripes. I don't go heavy, but enough that she'll feel a little sting, even through the jeans.

When I stop and rub, she hums in appreciation.

I reach around the front and unbutton her jeans, then shimmy them, along with her panties, down her legs. She kicks off her sneakers so I can get them off her feet. Then I slide my chair around behind her, push her ass open and lick her from behind.

Her pussy squeezes and ass clenches at the contact of my tongue with her sensitive lips. She shivers and trembles as I lick her from clit to anus and back again.

"Was this what you were hoping for when you said, *yes, please*?"

"Um, yes," she whimpers.

"You like the way I own your body, doll?"

"Yeah."

"Even though you kneed me in the balls for it?"

"I'm sorry," she pants. "I'm sorry about that."

"Tell me, angel." I stand to penetrate her with a finger. "What is it you're so afraid of?" I pump my finger inside her. "The way I make you feel? Or something you think I'm gonna do to you that you won't like?"

"I-I don't know," she gasps.

I pump faster, then stop to add a second finger and

pump again. "No, baby. I'm not accepting that answer." I keep pumping.

Her breath shudders, inner thighs tremble. She's close to coming just from my fingers.

"Tell me the fucking truth, Marissa." I push my thumb over the pucker of her asshole and rub.

Her pelvis jerks. She doesn't answer.

I pull my fingers out and slap her bare ass with a resounding crack.

"A-aah!"

"You want me to let you come, angel?"

She whimpers.

I slap her again. "Answer me with words."

"Yes, please."

"Then answer my question."

"It's not… I'm afraid because…"

I slap her again when she doesn't finish.

"Because you're a Tacone."

I wrap my fingers in her hair and tug her head up, lower mine to meet it. "So what?"

"So… you're dangerous."

I ignore the screwdriver that just rammed through my ribs. I push her hair back from her face so she can look into my eyes when I ask, "Dangerous to you?"

She blinks.

"Answer me," I murmur. "Am I dangerous to you, Marissa?"

After a moment, she tries to shake her head, which, of course, doesn't work because I'm holding her hair. "No," she whispers.

I release her hair. "No." I step back and slap her ass

again. "I'm gonna take care of you, Marissa. I told you that."

I pull out a condom and free my erection.

"Because of the nightmares?" she rasps.

The breath goes out of me at the mention of them. "Yeah—no—I don't know, baby. Because you're you. I'm not going to let anybody hurt you."

I slap her ass and hold, giving the plump cheek a jiggle. "Not even me."

I rub the head of my sheathed cock over her swollen entrance, and the flesh parts immediately to take me in. Like it's where I fucking belong.

The moment I'm in, I know I picked the wrong place for this. My glass table top will not withstand the pounding I want to give this girl. I slide in and out slowly, my eyes rolling back in my head with the glory of how good she feels. I grip her hips and give her a few short thrusts then a few slow full glides again.

"Angel, you want me to fuck you hard?"

"Yes." I love how there's no hesitation in her answer. She may be unsure of me in other ways, but my dominant kink doesn't scare her a bit.

In fact, I'd have to say Marissa's a bit of a freak in the sack, too.

"Then I'm gonna have to get you off this table or I'll crack it in two." I thrust in deep and pull her hips back with mine, helping her straighten. I rotate our bodies away from the table. "On your knees, *bella*." I pull out before she drops to her knees, but immediately follow her to the floor, thrusting in again the moment she's down.

And then it's just the bliss of slamming in and out.

117

Holding her hips firmly in place while I slap my loins against her ass, get in deep to satisfy the building need.

No telling how long I'm at it—my mind slipped away in the pleasure of it, but then it returns, and I realize I crave more.

I pull out. "On your back, doll. I want to see your face when I make you come."

Ever obedient, she instantly drops and wriggles onto her back before me, her knees bent open in an invitation.

"That's it, *bella*."

That's when I see she's shaved bare. Last time she was neatly trimmed. "Oh, angel. I stroke my thumb over the smooth skin. "Did you do this for me?"

She meets my gaze and holds it, nodding slowly.

Ave Maria.

She may not have worn the skirt, but she still was thinking about pleasing me. About giving herself to me. The shot of pleasure that runs through me nearly makes me come right there.

I spear her with my pulsing erection, slamming in and up hard.

She gasps and wraps her legs around my back.

"Baby, that definitely deserves a reward." I proceed to fuck her to high heaven. Every thrust gets me deeper, gets her wilder. She lets out panicked little cries, yanks my hips in with her ankles crossed behind my back. Digs her nails into my shoulders.

I love seeing her so lost, so crazed for the release.

It actually makes me hold out longer, my own pleasure so tied up in watching hers unfold. I shift my weight to one arm and use the other hand to roll and tweak one nipple. When I pinch it and hold, she comes with a scream.

"Gio! Oh my God! What are you doing to me?" Her hips buck frantically against mine as her pussy milks my cock.

I hold off a few more thrusts, and then I come too, shoving in deep and staying there for the release.

I drop my head into the crook of her shoulder, my breath combining with hers as we pant and recover. I suck her earlobe into my mouth, swirl my tongue around the delicate pink shell.

She squirms and giggles.

"*Che belleza*," I murmur against her skin. "I love watching you crash over the other side."

Her pussy squeezes, making my cock twitch inside her. "I've never had sex like this," she admits, which I'd already guessed.

"Me neither," I tell her. It's true. I've fucked a lot of girls. More than I'd ever care to count, and I've done it in every way imaginable, but it's all different with her. It feels new and exciting and so much better.

I brush her hair back from her face and trail my lips across hers in a loose, investigatory kiss. "You do something to me, Marissa. Something good."

"You make me feel…"

"What?" I prompt when she doesn't finish.

"I don't know. So much. Like everything's magnified —the good, the bad. All of it."

I ease out of her. "What's the bad, angel?" It's like one of those car crashes where you know what's coming but can't stop from asking.

She shakes her head. "No, it's not bad. Just my anxieties. I'm out of my depth with you, Gio. And it scares me."

I'm flayed open by her honesty. It makes me want to give her everything. My heart on a stick. My money. My life.

"Don't be scared with me," I murmur. "Never with me. Remember my promise? I'm a man of my word."

~

Marissa

I BLINK UP AT GIO, a riot of emotions filling my chest beyond capacity. It seems too unreal to believe this powerful, wealthy, dangerous man is making pledges to a twenty-five-year-old line cook from Cicero.

But if it all goes back to me being in his nightmares, I guess it makes sense. I represent something to him. Something about why he survived or what he should change in his second chance at life.

Because the moment is too big, too vulnerable, too scary, I blurt, "I made dessert."

A giant grin stretches across Gio's beautiful face. "She made me dessert," he narrates. "This girl is perfect." He arches one brow, movie-star style. "Only I thought you were the dessert, angel." He climbs off me and helps me to my feet.

"Another dessert, then," I tell him. I'm excited to give it to him. He was so stand-offish when I got here, I'd decided to just tuck it in the fridge and let him find it on his own, but now I'm eager to treat him.

"Lucky me," he rumbles.

"Yes," I agree.

"You're excited," he observes. "You really love what you do."

I try to pick up my jeans from the floor, but he swats my bare ass. "No clothing, angel. I like it when you serve me naked."

My well-used pussy gets hot and wet again at those words.

His gaze drops to my nipples, which tightened. Flushing, I scoot toward the kitchen and he follows me. When I try to at least put on the apron like last time, he shakes his head. "No way you're covering up that pretty pussy, angel."

"I think the health inspector might have something to say about this," I mutter, but I'm fighting a smile.

His smirk is sexy as hell.

I pull out the container with the dessert from the refrigerator and grab two plates. I keep my back to Gio as I dust the plates with powdered sugar and cocoa, then serve us each a piece of homemade tiramisu with a handcrafted espresso truffle on the side. I decorate the edges of the plates with a drizzle of raspberry sauce and one raspberry, one blackberry and one strawberry, cut into a flower shape. Then I turn to present them.

Gio's gaze falls on my body first, traveling from my breasts to my pussy and back to my breasts. Then he finally sees the dessert. "Tiramisu? My favorite."

"I remember," I admit. He always orders it when we

have it at the deli. "My nonna's recipe, but I made it special for you." I blush at the admission.

He holds his arm out. "Come here."

Setting down the plates, I walk over and he wraps his arm around my waist, pulling my naked body against his fully clothed one. His hand slides over my ass and squeezes.

"I fucking love it when you cook for me," he murmurs against my temple, then tips my chin up and slides his lips over mine in a slow kiss. "I might have to lower your wages so you never pay off your debt to me." He says it so warmly, with such an appreciative purr, the alarm bells don't go off in my head. "I guess you were right about the Tacones after all."

My pussy's dripping again. I don't know why my body's so responsive to him—whether it's his words or his touch, but I'm definitely owned, even without the money situation between us.

I look up and rub my nipples over his shirt. "Shouldn't you be making me an offer I can't refuse?"

The broad smile stretches his lips again, revealing gleaming white teeth. "Angel, I'd give you anything. Make a list and I'll start fulfilling it."

A puff of surprised laughter comes out of my mouth. "Okay... how about erasing my debt?" Might as well go for the gold, right?

Regret flickers over his face and my belly twists up tight. "Not that one, baby. I'm not ready to free the little caged bird yet."

I knew it was too much to ask—thirty grand is a huge debt to ask forgiveness for, and yet his refusal pierces me.

Maybe because he's so bald about what this is. I try to stumble back, but he holds me fast.

"We had a bargain, angel. We're both enjoying it. Let it ride a while longer, baby. I'm open to renegotiating if that changes.

I relax a little. He brings his mouth down, hovering over mine, but doesn't claim my lips. "Kiss me," he commands.

The moment I do, all my misgivings and apprehensions fall away. I wrap my arms around his neck. He pulls my legs up around his waist and I dive into everything it means to be owned by Gio Tacone. To be naked and at his mercy. He backs me against a wall and presses me into it, pinning me firmly so he can rub the bulge of his cock against my weeping pussy.

"Wh-what about dessert?" I gasp when he comes up for air.

"Spend the night," he demands.

I blink. The truth is, I had already told Aunt Lori I might not be home tonight. That I was going to a concert with a friend and would probably crash at her place. "Okay," I murmur.

Gio rewards me with his magnificent smile and slowly lets me slide to the floor. He kisses me one more time. "Then I guess we have time for dessert," he says, cupping my ass and giving it an appreciative squeeze before releasing me.

Gio picks up both plates and two spoons. "Pick a wine," he orders before carrying the plates out to the dining room.

I find a moscato dessert wine and pour it into small

crystal glasses. I love that Gio has every size and style in his cabinet. I hate to admit it, but I love everything about his luxury place. Just being in it makes me feel wealthy, as if being around the expensive furnishings somehow nourishes my own body and being.

In the living room, Gio pulls me onto his lap, straddling him, and feeds me the first bite. I take it, but as the delicious sweet confection melts in my mouth, I say, "You try it. I made it for you."

"I know, angel. I'm still rewarding you for that." I watch as he takes a bite and rolls his eyes with pleasure. "Mmm. So good, baby. I can taste the love you put into it."

I laugh. "That's what my nonna always says about her food."

"It's true." He feeds me another bite.

"So," I say, rolling the sweet, creamy fluff around in my mouth. "I haven't seen a piano move into Michelangelo's. What's going on with that?"

"Oh. Yeah. Still thinking about it."

I make a scoffing sound. "What's to think about? It's your dream, Gio. Make Michelangelo's into something you love. As long as you love it, so will the world. That's what one of my teachers at the culinary institute told us. She said yes, follow what's trending, know the market, know what's hot. But still create what you love."

Gio's gaze slides over to his baby grand.

"That piano in white would look perfect there," I insist. "Where do you get a piano like that? Let's go shopping tomorrow."

Gio's lips quirk. "You're gonna go piano shopping with me?"

"Yeah, totally. It will be fun."

"What time do you work?"

"I actually don't work tomorrow. Not at Michelangelo's and my aunt can probably handle Milano's—I've worked it alone all week with Mia's recovery. She owes me."

"That's great. It's my birthday."

"It is?" I straighten up. I'm the type who goes all out for birthdays. I don't know—product of being abandoned by my mom and hating every birthday growing up when she didn't show. Now I work overly hard to make sure everyone else's birthday isn't as big a disappointment as mine always are.

Gio feeds me the last bite of tiramisu and pops the truffle in his mouth. "*Ohhhhh* yeah. This is so good, angel. Coffee bean?"

I'm ridiculously pleased with his appreciation. "Espresso, yes."

"I love it."

I wriggle over his lap and put my arms around his neck. "What do you want me to make you for your birthday?"

His smile is feral. "Oh, angel. There's nothing you make that would disappoint me."

"That isn't what I asked. What's your favorite meal? Or dessert? Why didn't you tell me so I could make a special birthday dinner?"

He runs his hands up and down my bare back. "We do family dinner for birthdays. Will you come?"

I stop breathing.

I haven't even accepted the fact that Gio and I are

dating—or whatever we're doing. I'm so not ready to be brought to a birthday dinner with the family.

But Gio looks like he's holding his breath, too. And it's his birthday.

"You, um, really want me there, or you're just inviting me to be nice?"

I know he's not going to give the answer I'm hoping for. He brushes both my nipples with the pads of his thumbs at the same time, sending a shiver straight to my core. "I want you there. For my birthday present. Will you come?"

Fuck.

A Tacone family dinner.

I swallow. "Yeah. Okay. I'll go. On one condition."

"What's that?"

"You leave the gun at home."

It bothers the hell out of me that he wears a gun every time he leaves the house. Every time I see it or feel it on him, the memory of six dead bodies on the floor of Milano's shoots me through the center of my forehead.

He hesitates for a breath. "Yeah, okay."

"Okay?"

"Yeah." He shoots me that devastating grin. "Can I keep it in the car?"

"Leave the gun, take the cannoli," I joke, quoting *The Godfather,* but I also get wet. Is he really asking my permission? This man who rules Chicago. Who lives in a world of crime and violence? Whether it's a real power he's giving me, or just the illusion, I freaking love it. I kiss his neck. "That's a decent compromise."

Gio grins and pulls my hips tight against his. "Twenty-four hours with the girl of my dreams. Sounds like a perfect birthday."

"You mean nightmares," I say to take away the flutters in my belly, the panic over what I'm getting myself into.

His smile is sad. No—haunted. "Same thing."

CHAPTER 9

 io

MARISSA STARES DOWN at me from her perch on Michelangelo's bar. She's in her jeans and a blouse I bought her after she complained about not having clean clothes to wear. She still has that "just-fucked" look—flushed cheeks, glassy eyes, and a beautifully dazed expression, even though it's been a few hours. And that makes me want to fuck her all over again.

Cristo, I haven't had this much sex since I was in my twenties. Which I guess makes sense, since I'm with a twenty-something-year-old.

Last night I carried her to my bed and feasted on her pussy until she wept from the exhaustion of five orgasms. This morning she gave me a birthday blowjob, followed by breakfast in bed.

Then I took her to the piano store and let her pick out the baby grand for the restaurant. She picked a gleaming white beauty which I paid double for to get them to drop everything and deliver it today. So after I took her to lunch at one of the most expensive restaurants in Chicago, we went to Michelangelo's to meet the piano movers.

Now it's installed in the corner, and I played her my best rendition of *The Scientist* by Coldplay, and I broke into the wine. I push her knees wide and bite the seam of her jeans between her legs. "I want this pussy again."

She looks down at me.

I never would've guessed Marissa would be this freaky, but she gives me this wide smile and says, "You're the boss."

Jesus fucking Christ. She makes my dick hard on a moment-to-moment basis.

"All that resistance, angel, and then you suddenly surrender. Explain it to me."

She tenses and I regret bringing it up.

I massage her inner thighs with my thumbs to loosen her back up. " Never mind," I say. "I don't fucking care. I like you willing." I grip her waist and tug her down to her feet. With a flick, I unbutton her jeans and shove my hand down the front. She's sopping wet. Like a dripping peach, only slick and soft. I spin her around so her ass comes to my front to get a better angle, and I find her clit with my finger. She squirms, dropping her head back on my shoulder. I curl a finger inside her, grinding the heel of my hand over her clit while I dip a second finger in.

Marissa covers my hand with hers and urges me deeper. I walk her forward, my fingers still inside her. Her thighs bump into a four-top and she folds over it, catching herself with her hands. I shove her jeans down and slap her ass.

"Do you have any idea how hot this is, angel?" I ask as I spread her ass cheeks to take in the full sight of her. "Ah, what am I saying? Every time with you is hot." I rub over her wet folds again, then release my cock. I can't get the condom on fast enough.

Now I know why men find a younger woman after their midlife crisis. I've never felt so alive as I have these last eighteen hours. It's fucking invigorating. But no, it's not because Marissa's younger. It's that she's *Marissa*. She could be the older one, and I'd still find her fuck-all hot. I'd still want to bang her five times a day.

I ease into her welcoming pussy, and she moans. "You bending over and taking it from your boss, pretty girl? Eh *bella*?" I can't stop the filth from pouring from my mouth. Fortunately, Marissa doesn't seem to find it degrading. She moans, reaching back and pulls her ass cheeks apart for me. I bump her ass with my loins, grinding against her anus so she gets that added titillation. I go slow, watching the root of my cock disappear into her welcoming entrance and come out glistening.

I haven't even come yet, and I'm already grateful. When she starts murmuring my name in that hoarse, urgent way, my control snaps, and I have to give it to her hard. I grip her hips and slam in and out, shaking the table with the force.

The angle's good, but I want to be deeper in her. And I want to see her face. Last night has me addicted to watching her come. I pull out and lift her bare ass onto the tablecloth, then climb on top, one foot braced on a chair, one knee on the table.

Marissa's giggle turns to a sex cry as I plow into her, using my foot on the chair for better leverage. It's a brutal, dominating fuck, but she doesn't complain, not even when I get fast and rough.

I try to slow down and remember her pleasure, but my own need overwhelms me. I'm senseless with desire.

"Gio... Gio." When she starts that hoarse chanting of my name again, I come like a rocket blast, and it's not until I've shot my load and am still stroking in and out in sheer bliss that my mind returns. I pinch one of her nipples, hard. "Come for me, angel."

She does. Right on cue like her body was made to be commanded by me. The surge of power that rushes through me makes me come some more. Or maybe it's the way her tight muscles milk my dick for every last drop of cum.

I ease out of her and off the table because I know it can't be the most comfortable position. "My compliments to Michael on his tables," I say, giving the surface a shake. "Very sturdy."

She lets out a shaky laugh. "Gio, I don't have all that much experience, but I'm pretty sure you're ruining sex with other men for me."

I have to turn away to hide the flare of possessive jealousy that floods through me at those words. "Pretty sure that's the point," I manage to say. I dispose of my condom in the trash. When I return, I help her off the table and use one of the cloth napkins to clean up.

And then I can't stop myself. "Don't mention other

men to me, angel. I bought a whole restaurant to keep one man's hands off you. If I hear of another, I'm not sure I'll be so gracious."

She stares at me with wide doe-eyes. I can't tell if she's pissed or scared, or just stunned.

"You really did, didn't you?"

"You still don't believe me?"

Her nod wobbles. "I'm beginning to," she whispers.

I grip her jaw and taste her lips and she opens to me, a flower willing to bloom.

Marissa

I'M NOT sure I even recognize myself.

Gio cracked open this whole sexual side of me I didn't know existed. And now that she's out, I don't know how to put her away.

I don't *want* to put her away.

I love the way Gio makes me feel—like I'm the center of the universe.

Being abandoned by my mom as a child left scars on me. The kind that tell me I have to work extra hard to be worthy of love or affection. The kind that instilled fear of not being good enough.

Those fears are still present, maybe even more so, because I'm afraid of getting used to this feeling—to being important to someone. Celebrated, even.

But this is just sex. I have to remember that. Gio's a player and this is probably how he plays.

He bought a restaurant for you.

I draw in a breath. He bought an entire restaurant—just for me. That's not playing.

We strip the tablecloth from the table where he just owned me, and I set it with a new one and then it's time to go to his birthday dinner.

He locks up and takes me by the hand, lacing his fingers with mine as he leads me to his SUV. "Don't be nervous," he says, even though I was trying to hide my mood. "My family's easy. It will be just another loud Italian family gathering. Lots of food and talking over each other." He winks at me, and I melt a little.

I want to believe him, but this is where my bias against his family comes in again. They're the Tacones. The notorious crime family that held Milano's hostage for forty years. The family responsible for six dead bodies on our floor last year.

"Will Junior be there?" I try to make the question casual, but Gio slides his gaze over and eyes me speculatively. He's too perceptive sometimes.

"Yeah." He opens my car door and helps me in.

I draw in a shaky breath, wishing I'd made an excuse for dinner.

But no, it's Gio's birthday and he wants me there.

And that's the part that gets me.

He wants me there.

It's a strange and foreign feeling, and one I like way too much.

We don't talk much on the way to his mother's. I fidget with my purse strap and the radio.

"Should I be more dressed up?" I blurt when it suddenly occurs to me that the Tacones are rich, and I'm showing up in jeans.

"Stop," Gio cuts in immediately. "You look perfect. No one's gonna judge you, angel. They'll be delighted I brought a girl."

That news calms me down. I steal a sidelong glance at him. "You don't usually?"

He flashes that panty-melting grin. "Never, doll. I was the consummate bachelor."

I try to ignore the tingle of pleasure at the back of my neck, running down my arms. I'm special to Gio. More evidence that it's true.

The news makes me bold enough to push for more. "And now?"

Gio's grin widens. "Now I'm about you, little girl. Or hadn't you figured that out, yet?"

My face flushes with pleasure and a bit of embarrassment that I just fished for that information.

"I've been trying to hold back—not to come on too strong, especially because you seem to have some hangups with me. But standing back and waiting isn't my style, doll. I think I've shown remarkable restraint. But that shit is over. Consider my intentions declared."

My pussy tingles at his declaration. Gio's dirty talk is off the charts hot, but this? Real relationship talk from a tough guy mafia man? I've never been so turned on in my life.

I swallow. "Noted."

Gio smirks as he parks in front of a lovely suburban Victorian and gets out. I push my door open and draw a deep breath. I can do this. I'm with Gio and he's all about me. That pretty much makes any situation navigable, doesn't it?

He stops right before we go in. "Hey, my ma doesn't know anything about me getting shot, and I want to keep it that way, okay?"

Shock ripples through me. How did he keep something so big from her? And he seems so open with me, but what is he keeping from me?

We walk in the door, and his mother comes flying out of the kitchen, her arms stretched wide. "Gio!" Her expression turns to delighted surprise when she sees me. "You brought a girl!"

"Gio brought a girl?" I hear a man's voice ask from the living room, and then family descends from all directions.

"Ma, this is Marissa, Marissa Milano. She owns the cafe Pops used to go to in Cicero."

"I remember hearing about it." Gio's mother kisses both my cheeks. "Welcome, welcome. I'm so glad you came to help Gio celebrate his birthday."

His brother Paolo gives me the double-cheek kisses, too. "Good to see you, Marissa."

I have the same visceral reaction to seeing Junior I have every time since the shooting. Ice flushes over me, and the memory of him pointing his pistol at my head floods back. I force a smile and offer my face for his kisses, too, and he introduces me to his beautiful Latina wife, Desiree, and their baby Santo and son Jasper.

"Junior, can we have a word?" Gio says, picking up my hand and squeezing it.

Wait… what? Does *we* include me? Because I'd rather keep my distance from Junior.

But Junior agrees, shooting a speculative look over his shoulder as he leads us to a study. Gio shuts the door behind us, and I stand there shaking, wanting to run.

"You owe Marissa an apology," Gio says immediately.

Oh fuck.

I start shaking harder. So hard Gio notices and pulls me against his side.

"Yeah?" Junior is scary as hell. As scary as Don Tacone, the patriarch of the family. He turns those dark eyes on me.

I can't breathe. I mean not at all. I stand there, unable to inhale or exhale. Or even move, other than tremble.

"Yeah. For pointing a gun at her. You scared her, Junior. She has nightmares."

I want to kill Gio for exposing me like this. I thought I handled the shooting pretty well in the moment. When the *bratva* bastards came in and camped out at every table in the cafe, I'd tried to warn Junior it was a trap.

But then it was too late, and their leader shot Gio on the sidewalk out front. And I covered up for them afterward. Lied to the police and told them it was all *bratva*. No Sicilians involved at all.

Junior absorbs this news and drops his head to the side. "Aw, Marissa. I'm sorry. It all happened so fast. You moved, I aimed. I thought you were one of them, that's all. I would never hurt you. You gotta believe that."

Some of my backbone returns. I lift my chin. "You

thought about shooting," I accuse. "Even after you saw it was me."

Gio turns his gaze on his brother and raises his brows. "That true?"

Junior meets my gaze and holds it. He shakes his head. "I would never do it, Marissa. We don't harm the innocent."

To my horror, tears fill my eyes. "He told you to," I mumble through trembling lips. It feels good to get it out. To talk about the moment I haven't shared with a single soul.

"Who did?" Gio demands.

"Luca," Junior mutters. He remembers. We all three will probably remember that evening until the day we die.

She's a witness, his henchman said, and I'd had no choice but to beg for my life.

"Luca's job is to warn me of danger. But I knew you weren't a threat to me. You aren't, are you, Marissa?"

There's a slight warning to Junior's tone, and Gio instantly growls, "Watch it."

Junior holds up his hands. "No, no. All I'm saying is that it's absurd to believe I'd ever want to hurt her." He turns to me. His expression is gentle. It's one I haven't seen on him before. "You tried to warn me that day, didn't you?"

I nod, mutely.

"I'm grateful to you, Marissa. And I'm sorry if you think I would ever pull that trigger on you. I wouldn't. I swear to *La Madonna.*"

I'm still shaking, but I can breathe again. I manage a nod of acceptance.

Gio tips my chin to look at me. "Yeah? You believe him?"

Do I? I'm not sure. I want to, yes. I nod.

"Feel better?" Gio presses, like he's going to take some action on my behalf if I don't.

I elbow him away. "Jesus, Gio. You didn't have to go and make a big thing about it. Now I'm embarrassed."

"No," he says, waving his hands in that distinctly Italian way. "This matters. I want you coming around here, seeing my family. And I can't have you scared every time you see my brother."

Junior shoots Gio a curious glance before he extends his hand. "No, I definitely don't want you scared of me. Please." When I place my hand in his, he covers it with his other one and squeezes, holding me captive. "Accept my apologies. For everything that went down that night."

I blink. I know my lips are still trembling, so I don't trust myself to talk. It's funny how far an apology goes.

Much farther than the money. The Tacones took care of us after the shooting. Paolo had the windows replaced the following day and Junior gave me twice as much cash as it cost to repair everything.

But hearing him say he's sorry in plain words makes a difference. A large chunk of the fear and anger I've been holding on to against the Tacones as a result of that day breaks off and floats away.

"Thanks," I manage to say after a moment, cursing my voice for wobbling.

But Junior releases my hand and draws me in for a hug, like we're family. And I don't mind. It's nice, actually.

When he lets me go, Gio pulls my back against his front and wraps his arms around me from behind. He kisses my hair. "You okay?"

"Yeah."

Junior peers down at me. "You sure?"

I nod again. "Yeah. Thanks."

"Okay. Let me know if there's anything I can do for you or your family, Marissa," Junior says. It makes me think he doesn't know about the loan Gio already gave me. So it was off the books, like Gio promised.

"Thanks, Mr. Tacone—Junior."

We file out of the den and into the chaos of a noisy family gathering, and something in me I didn't know I was holding relaxes. Some space opens up in my chest for more breath.

The din of chatter soothes me and my nerves ebb. Maybe Gio's right. They are just like any other family.

Gio

IT WAS everything I could do not to bash my brother's face in when I felt Marissa trembling beside me. I think Junior must've recognized the depth of my rage, because he was uncommonly kind. Or maybe he's just changed.

Desiree and fatherhood have given him a new lease on life.

I had no idea how much Marissa still suffers from having that gun pointed at her, although I should have realized. Her hands shook the day I came into the cafe. I thought it was because I startled her. But no, her PTSD is as bad as mine—that's why she recognized the signs in me.

We all gather in the kitchen to eat antipasto from a platter while my mom and Junior finish dinner.

Everyone keeps shooting curious glances at my date. They will be asking me about her for an eternity now, but I don't give a shit. I wanted her here. She makes me feel alive for the first time in years.

I keep her close to my body, my arm draped loosely around her waist. It's a signal to my family that she's absolutely under my protection, not that I expect anyone to offend her. There's more ease in our family gatherings than ever before, but old habits die hard.

Dinner is my favorite—stuffed shells with homemade sausage. Marissa is a sweetheart, exclaiming over the food and cleaning her plate, despite the fact that it's not the gourmet cuisine she likes to make.

She fits in, though. She joins the noisy conversation. Talks to Desiree and my mom. To Jasper. She has that ease with the family that Desiree did from the start. I know it's nuts—way too fucking soon—but I fantasize about making this permanent. Putting a big shiny ring on her finger and keeping her forever.

But I know I'm way ahead of myself. She only just let her defenses down in bed. She's still pretty damn far from allowing me into the rest of her life.

"Is it time for cake?" Jasper asks the moment I clean my plate.

"Is there cake?" I feign surprise.

"Yes!" He jumps out of his chair. "Chocolate cake with raspberry filling. Nonna made it."

My mother beams. She loves that the boy already calls her Nonna, like she's been his grandmother his whole life. "Well, I think we'd better get the plates cleared so we can have cake. Can you help, Jasper?" I hand him mine and he cruises into the kitchen with it.

Marissa tries to get up, but I pull her back down. "Sit with me, angel."

"Why don't you play something on the piano while we clean up?" my mom suggests.

"Yes," Marissa agrees. "Why don't you?"

It's an old routine, but it feels new with Marissa here. I take her hand and pull her with me to the piano. It's my first piano—the one my mom badgered my dad into getting me. My oldest friend.

I sit down and consider Marissa. Then I smile when I think of what to play. I start playing and singing one of the first love songs I learned to play—*She's Always a Woman*, by Billy Joel. I sing it right to Marissa, who blushes and nibbles her plump lower lip. By the time I finish, the rest of the family has gathered.

"Who sings that?" Marissa asks. Of course it was way before her time.

"Billy Joel," I say, playing the start of *Piano Man* in homage.

"The piano man, himself," Paolo says with a derisive edge to his voice. "There was a time when little Gio dreamed of playing in piano bars just like old Billy, didn't you?" He laughs and slaps me on the back.

"And why shouldn't he, if that was his dream?"

Marissa challenges. She levels her gaze at Paolo like she's daring him to make fun of me.

My lips twitch.

The rest of the family blink in surprise.

"Yeah, I'm, uh…" Why is it so fucking hard to tell them? I still feel like it's this shameful, embarrassing thing.

Junior hones in on it. "Are you playing publicly, Gio?" He sounds surprised, but not judgmental.

"Yeah. Well, I'm thinking about it. See, I bought this restaurant."

"What?" My ma says loudly. "You bought a restaurant? Why didn't you tell me about this?"

"What restaurant?" Paolo demands.

"It's called Michelangelo's. Marissa's a chef there and, uh, yeah. We moved a piano in today."

"No shit." Junior sounds stunned.

"Language, Junior," my mother chides. "I think it's wonderful, Gio. When do you play? I'll come every night."

I laugh. "Please don't, Ma. And I haven't started yet. Still in the planning phase."

"Good for you," Junior says, and I have no indication he doesn't mean it.

Paolo's still looking at me like I have two heads, and he's clearly keeping his mouth shut because he can't say anything nice. Well, fuck him.

I lift my hands and drop them on the keys again, playing my best rendition of The Beatles' *Birthday*, singing and hamming it up to make Jasper laugh.

When I get up from the bench, I knit my fingers

through Marissa's and lean down to murmur "thank you" in her ear. When she turns her face up to mine, I steal a quick kiss from her. "You really are an angel."

"Gio," she murmurs, her intelligent eyes trained on mine. She's searching for something, but I can't tell what.

"I'd do anything for you, doll," I tell her in a low voice as we head back to the dining room for cake.

Her intake of breath gives me shivers. Her expression is a mixture of fear and hope. Again, I'm not sure how to decipher it.

I think she's deciding whether to give me her heart.

CHAPTER 10

io

ALL GOOD THINGS must come to an end, and my twenty-four hours with Marissa landed with a thud when she made me drop her around the corner from her grandparents' place instead of walking her to the door.

She may fit in perfectly with my family, but I'm definitely not the guy she can bring home to Grandma.

Fuck.

Well, that's a problem I'll have to figure out. And I'm sure I can. Nico might have some ideas. I'm sure as hell not going to ask Junior. He's a big part of the problem.

I didn't give in to the temptation to get up into Marissa's business today. I'm content tonight to sit at the restaurant and watch things run, knowing she's just behind that kitchen door. Remembering that I just had her yesterday, bent over the table by the wall.

Michael wanted to shit all over the piano when he saw it. "Fine dining is in silence," he told me more than once. I let him grouse for a few minutes, and then I told him to shut the fuck up.

He did. The guy's scared of me, which suits me fine.

It's remembering Marissa's enthusiasm when I played last night—defending me to my brother, Paolo, that finally moves me to get up from my seat in the corner of Michelangelo's and walk to the baby grand. It's 10:00 p.m. The dinner crowd is winding down. This place needs a little music. It's way too fucking quiet.

I sit down and start to play a sweet version of Leonard Cohen's *Hallelujah*. There's a moment of surprise when I begin and then the room settles into the notes. The customers accept the music and let it move through them, enhance their experience of the food, wine and company. I don't know how the fuck I know that, but that's my sense, anyway. That's how I experience music.

I play for an hour and the people stay at their tables, buying more wine or coffee, ordering dessert. Even though Michael's frowning his ass off in the corner, I know it was a success. I feel the vibe, and the vibe is good. People are happy. They're spending more money. They're staying to hear me play.

And for a guy who's never performed publicly but always longed for the give-and-take that comes from a live audience, I'm floating.

And I have Marissa Milano to thank for it.

When I start to catch dirty looks from the servers, I

stop playing. They want to go home. I get it. We'll have to figure out a better routine. Maybe a change or reduction of staff after the music starts.

I order a scotch and settle back in my corner, watching the servers clean up. Waiting for Marissa.

I didn't contact her today. We don't have an arrangement to meet up after her shift. I don't know, maybe this is a test. I'm trying to figure out if she's accepted she's mine or if I have to keep pursuing. And is it time to go in hard?

This holding back and letting things roll on her time is about to kill me.

Marissa

"You let him have it, didn't you?" Lilah asks when I dawdle at closing time.

Henry was an even bigger asshole tonight, I guess because we don't have a replacement for Arnie yet. He stormed out without a goodbye ten minutes ago. The dishwasher just left and all the servers are gone.

Out in the restaurant, the sounds of the piano start up again.

Whatever Lilah sees in my face confirms it. "I knew it!" She thrusts her fist in the air like it's a victory. She's been pressing me ever since Arnie disappeared for the scoop, and I've been trying to play it off like I don't know anything. "Was he good? Is he good?"

I can't stop the smile from spreading across my face.

"So good. Older man with a shit-ton of experience and five times as much testosterone good."

She grabs my hands and squeezes them. "Ooh! I'm so excited for you. Come a little extra hard for me."

"Shut up." I slap her hands away lightly. I know I'm blushing. And excited. Just knowing Gio was on the other side of the kitchen door all night had me all aflutter. Hearing him play piano thrilled me.

Now I just can't wait to see him.

"See if you can get us a raise," she teases as she heads to the door.

"Already did," I say. I was going to let it be a surprise, but since she mentioned it…

Lilah stops. "What? Are you kidding me?"

I grin. "Nope. Three bucks an hour."

Lilah jumps up and down, running back to grab my hands again. "Are you serious? That's like"—she lifts her eyes while calculating in her head—"almost an extra five hundred a month."

I bob my head. I'd already done the math myself. "I know."

She turns me and gives me a shove. "Well go and *thank* him for me." She waggles her brows.

I laugh. "I will." Stomach in flutters, I push the door to the restaurant open and head out. Most of the lights are off. No one's left but Gio, sitting at the piano.

I go to his side, intending to sit beside him on the bench, but he stops playing and pulls me onto his lap instead.

The sense of rightness is undeniable. Now that I've mostly let go or ignored my qualms about getting in a relationship with Gio, everything feels right. The pleasure at the way he manhandles me—like a possession, like an object. With total confidence. Not asking. Just taking.

I thought I would hate to be treated this way.

But I freaking love it. To be this wanted.

Especially because I do believe that Gio respects me. Respects my agency.

"Come home with me," he murmurs against my neck.

I groan. "I can't." I have to work tomorrow morning at Milano's because Mia starts physical therapy and my grandparents are in Boston for a cousin's wedding.

"You gonna let me fuck you here, then?" he rasps. His words are crass, but his hands rove over my body, making it sing.

"Yes," I answer immediately.

I can't wait to have sex with him again. Every single time has rocked my world. I meant it when I said he ruined other men for me. Like, I seriously don't see how any other man on the planet could compare.

He cups my pussy now, rubbing through my pants. I shift and grind my ass over his hardened cock. "Don't fucking tease, baby. I've been hard for you all night, just knowing you were back there in the kitchen with that banging body." He bites my neck. "This body that belongs to me."

"Yes," I agree, squirming against his touch.

"Suck my cock, angel. Show me you're a good girl."

Holy shit. Those words should totally offend me, but instead, they set my world on fire. I instantly slide to the floor and sit on my heels, waiting eagerly for him to take out his manhood.

I may not have that much experience, but I do know how to give a good blowjob. I started young and learned early the power I could wield with my mouth. How it let me off the hook from having sex before I was ready. How it made me wanted. Keepable.

I grip the base of his cock firmly, making it jut out to meet my mouth, and I start by licking all around the head.

Gio's breath grows ragged before I even take him down my throat. Then he gets rough. He wraps his fist in my hair and takes over, controlling my head to pull me on and off his cock. I notice he's careful not to go too deep, which I appreciate, because it is slightly frightening to give up total control this way.

I massage his balls, move my fingers farther back and massage his taint, looking for the prostate.

"Oh, angel. It's so good. It's so good, and it's not enough. I always want to be inside you."

He pulls me off and stares down at me with bald hunger.

"Was I a good girl?" I don't know what possesses me to say it—in what universe I became the sex kitten, but flames flare in his eyes.

"So fucking good," he grates, dropping to his knees in front of me. "Pants off. Get those legs over my shoulders."

Oh. My. *Gawd.*

I scramble to shuck my shoes, pants and panties while Gio rolls a condom over his dick. When I drop to my back on the freshly vacuumed carpet, he picks up my legs and props them over his shoulders.

"Are you wet for me, Marissa?" He rubs his thumb over my weeping slit, testing my readiness. I'm ripe and swollen for him and he groans as he brings his thumb to his mouth and sucks off my juices.

"You gonna come out here every night and suck my dick at the end of your shift?" He rubs the head of his cock over my clit a few times before spearing me with his erection.

"Yes," I whisper. And that promise doesn't feel like one ounce of hardship. I like the way it feels to be used by Gio.

He holds the tops of my thighs and fucks me fast and hard. "It's not enough," he snarls, surprising me.

And my own reaction surprises me even more.

The need to please him.

We've taken these roles. He's in charge. I'm his property. I submit to his authority.

"I want you in my bed. Why can't I have you in my bed, Marissa?" He's plowing into me so fast and hard, I can't think. Can't figure out how to answer him.

"Gio," I whimper.

"Come home with me." It's not a question. It's a demand.

And yet there's entreaty in his eyes.

His tactics may be to strong-arm me, but we're still negotiating. I could say no.

"I-I have to work in the morning. At Milano's," I pant.

"I'll drive you."

And then I'm suddenly overwhelmed. Tears spear my eyes. I close them so he won't see. "Yes, okay." My cry is hoarse.

Gio roars and pounds into me hard, all his victory channeled into his release. He comes and my muscles instantly seize around his length, his body truly is the master of mine. He pushes in tight and stays there. My channel squeezes and milks his cock in waves of delicious release. When I finally stop, Gio rocks back and in a few more times and pulls out.

"Marissa?"

I still haven't opened my lids. The concern in his voice makes me reluctantly pry them open now. Tears spill down my temples toward the floor.

"Oh, fuck, baby. Did I hurt you?"

I shake my head.

"What'd I do?" He thumbs away my tears on one side. "You don't have to come home with me. I didn't mean it, angel. I'm a dick, *bambina*. I'm sorry."

I shake my head. "No, it's not that." My voice wobbles.

"Baby, *tell* me. Did I hurt you? Was I too rough?"

"You were perfect," I say quickly to stop his line of thought. "You always are."

He cradles my cheek in his hand. The gesture is infinitely gentle, the tenderness in contrast to his usual firm, controlling touch. "What is it?" The alarm still shines bright in his eyes.

I swallow. "It just… feels good."

He drops his head to the side to study me. "What does?"

"To be so wanted. It just feels good, that's all." I push myself up to sit, embarrassed of my tears.

Gio catches my face in his hands. "Who ever made you feel unwanted?" And then he guesses, "That bitch of a mom of yours?"

I wince, but nod, wondering how he knows. But he's been hanging out at Milano's since he was a kid. He probably remembers when I suddenly showed up—the abandoned daughter of a drug-addicted mom.

He shakes his head. "Stupidest thing she ever did was run off on you." His expression turns to one of chagrin. "Hell, all I ever want to do is run after you. And I'm getting tired of holding myself back."

I manage a watery smile. "I have to admit, I like being chased. Way too much."

Gio pulls me into him, straddling his lap. "Is that why you keep running?" There's a serious edge to his voice that tears right through my defenses. Shreds the thin walls of the tent I'm camped in.

"No," I admit.

He runs his hands up and down my back. "Then why? Because I'm a Tacone?"

I drop my forehead against his chest. I don't want to admit it. I know it will hurt him. He may be a badass Family man, but he takes offense easily—at least with me he does. "I'm sorry, Gio," I whisper.

"Look at me," he commands.

I don't want to.

I *really* don't want to.

But he waits until I lift my head and meet his gaze.

"I can't help the family I was born into. And I can't change what I've been. The things I've done. But I want you to know things are different now. Our dad is in jail. Nico's made us a fortune with a legitimate casino/hotel business. And after the *bratva* shit went down last year, Junior shut down all our remaining business in Chicago."

153

He lifts his arms as if to show me his waist. "Look—I left the gun in the car. I let your boss live, angel. I've changed. I almost died last year. And I've had a real hard time figuring out the point of living since then. But now I think I found it."

My gaze flicks to the piano, but he catches my chin and pulls it back to him. "No, not the piano. Although that's wonderful, too. No, it's you, baby. You're bringing me back to life. That must be why I kept dreaming about you. *La Madonna* was showing me where life was worth living."

I burst into messy tears, and Gio pulls me up against him tight. I wrap my arms around his neck with a strangulating hold.

"I'm keeping you, baby. I just gotta figure out how to get you on board with that."

"I'm on board." I sniff against his neck. "Yeah, I'm on board. Take me to your place, Gio."

io

I DON'T WANT to wake Marissa. Her face is so soft and innocent and she's only had five hours of sleep. But she has to open at Milano's, and I said I'd get her there.

Still, I don't move. I just drink in the sight of her. I had the nightmare again. Woke in a cold sweat from the horror of seeing her with a gun at her head.

But she's right here. In my bed. Safe and sound.

Where I want to keep her always. Where she belongs. I just have to figure out how to convince her of that.

I trail kisses along her hairline. "Wake up, angel. We have to get going."

"Hmm? Mmm." Her lids flutter, but she slips right back into slumber.

"I wish the fuck I could let you sleep, doll, but I promised you I'd get you to Milano's on time."

"Hmm?" She sits up at the word *Milano's*. "Oh. Yeah. Thanks." Her smile is sweet and fucking gracious. I want to kiss her, but if I do, I'll be holding her down and feasting between her legs for the next hour, and there's no time for that.

"I'm sorry, *bella*. I hate to wake you."

"No, it's good." She pushes a limp hand through her hair. "Thank you."

I hand her the latte I paid the doorman to fetch and help her out of bed.

"Gio." I love the way her voice is husky with sleep. "You're so good to me. Thank you."

"Get used to it, baby," I tell her, giving her bare, beautiful ass a light slap when she stands. "I keep trying to spoil you. Are you ready to finally let me?"

She stops trying to step into her jeans and blinks at me. "Yes."

I cup her chin and give her a light kiss. "Good girl." I leave the room to keep from distracting her from getting dressed. When she emerges, we head downstairs together, my fingers laced through hers.

I like the way this feels. Being in charge of Marissa. Waking her up, getting her where she needs to be. I've never had someone to care for before. Never wanted that. That's why I didn't look for the wife and family deal.

But this—it feels so right. So good.

I drive her to Milano's, trying to figure out how I can help. The girl works too hard. And I'm a bastard, because I want more of her time.

"So, Milano's. What would it take for you to be able to quit?"

She sighs as she twists her hair on the top of her head with a scrunchie. "Mia growing up to help my aunt run it."

I snort. "And Mia's what? Eight years old?"

"Yes."

I shake my head. "You gotta think outside the box, baby. You believe there's only one way to end your servitude. It was like me thinking violence was the only way to handle your dickwad boss. I needed someone else's perspective to see there are other options available. Maybe I could provide that for you."

She shakes her head. "I don't know, Gio. I've been trying to find my way out of this jail for a long time. I love my grandparents. I owe them everything. And Milano's is their only livelihood. They don't own the building, so it's not like they can sell and retire on the equity. The neighborhood's gone to shit, so getting new customers or new investors has proven difficult. We don't make enough to even pay someone else minimum wage. And my grandparents don't have much social security because they barely paid into the system. Besides, we can't shut down Milano's, because it's my aunt's livelihood, too."

"Your aunt could find another job and make just as much," I remind her. "If you're not even paying yourselves minimum wage, she'd actually do better somewhere else.

"That's true. But she couldn't set her own hours. Take off when she needs to."

"Yeah, but her taking off means you have to cover her shift. So I'm not seeing that as a selling point to staying open."

Marissa's shoulders slump even more.

I reach over and squeeze her knee. "Don't worry. There's gonna be some other solution. We just gotta solve your grandparents' retirement."

"And convince them it's time to retire—yes."

It seems easy to me. I just offer to buy the business for way more than it's worth. But if I understand correctly, Luigi—who we thought was a friend all these years—actually hates the Tacones. So the chance of me making this end happily is greatly diminished.

"I'll work on it," I tell her.

She shoots me a suspicious glance. "Please don't do anything crazy without consulting me first? My grandparents are... set in their ways."

"Is that code for your grandparents hate me?"

She winces. "Kind of."

Fuck.

I gotta get this Tacone problem solved. If I want Marissa for keeps, I have to make peace with her grandparents. Otherwise, I may never convince her I'm worthy.

"You can just drop me in front," she says, but I ignore her and park the SUV. I take her keys from her hand to unlock the doors and walk her in, checking the corners for intruders, then trailing her to the kitchen. When she takes the dishes of food out of the walk-in to place in the display case, I do the same.

"What are you doing?"

"Helping you open the place," I say, even though it seems pretty obvious.

Once more, she stops in place, and blinks back tears. "Are you fucking kidding me?"

"Hey." I shake my head. "No more tears. I told you to get used to it. I have your back. I'm here for you. *Capiche*?"

She keeps blinking rapidly. "'Kay," she says softly. Then lets out a watery laugh. "You're so unexpected, Gio."

She finishes putting the food out and puts on a pot of coffee to brew, then unlocks the door to customers. I sit in the corner when a few older men come in—obviously regulars because they call her by name. She brings them out their food.

I read the newspaper without seeing it, still working on the problem of winning over Luigi.

Marissa appears in front of me with a steaming espresso and a slice of bacon, egg and cheese strata on a plate.

"Mmm." I wrap my arm around her waist and tug her closer. "I like it when you serve me," I murmur, low enough that no one else can hear.

"I like it when you make me," she murmurs back, then slaps a hand over her mouth.

I flash her a knowing smile, remembering how I ordered her on her knees last night. How excited she got about giving me a blowjob. She does like to be owned by me. With just a little more trust between us, she'll surrender to those desires completely, knowing I'll never abuse the honor of being her owner and protector.

"You don't have to blush when you tell me how you like it, angel," I murmur, even lower, letting her know I understand we're talking sex, here.

The blush spreads across her chest and up her neck. Her nipples protrude, visible even beneath her bra.

159

I squeeze her hip and release her before the other customers get curious. "What time are you off?"

She shakes her head. "My aunt promised to be back in time for me to be able to take a shower and get to Michelangelo's for my shift."

Damn. My girl works way too hard.

I have to get this figured out for her.

CHAPTER 12

$\mathcal{M}$ arissa

"DON'T THINK you're not in big trouble," Gio rumbles, catching me around the waist when I enter his apartment with my cart of food.

I'm late. And I had to reschedule because I got called into Michelangelo's yesterday on my day off.

God help me, I like being in trouble with him.

Over the past two weeks, we've had crazy mad sex. Sex every day, multiple times and it's always good. But my favorite times are when he's a little annoyed or frustrated with me. When I tell him I can't spend the night, or I push him away emotionally.

That's when he gets more aggressive. More dominant. A little punitive. It's when he spanks my ass red and drills me hard. When his hold is rough and his passion fiery hot.

It's a strange paradox though. I like when he's mad, but

161

I don't like displeasing him. I don't want him to be genuinely annoyed with me. Or hurt.

I turn into the circle of his arms and peer up at him. "I'm sorry," I murmur in my best sex kitten voice. "You can punish me for it later." I bite his chin.

His arm tightens around me, and I watch his hazel eyes flood to black as his pupils dilate. "Damn straight I'll punish you." His cock hardens against my belly. "I'm gonna punish you all night. Come here, baby."

He throws me over his shoulder.

"Ack! Gio!" I shriek and giggle as he carries me to the bedroom. "Aren't you hungry?"

"I'm always hungry, angel. For you, for your food. For this pussy." He tosses me down on the bed and yanks my skirt up to my waist. "Oh fuck, *bambina*."

I wore a skirt and heels because I know he likes it when I dress up for him, and tonight I have on black thigh-highs.

Gio rubs his stubbled jaw. "That is too fucking sexy." He trails his palms up the outsides of my legs. "This goes a long way toward forgiveness, angel."

Heat's building between my legs and I'm already squirming. He slips one thumb under the hem of my panties, brushing the very top of my thigh. "And the panties match. What about the bra?"

He's suddenly gentle as he works the delicate buttons on my blouse, but once it's open, he throws it wide. "Fuck, yeah."

They match. Everything's black satin and lace.

"You're lucky you're so beautiful, babygirl. You know that? You're as pretty as they come."

I roll my hips on the bed, hungry for his touch. "Why am I lucky?"

His grin is wicked. "Because I hardly want to mark your skin."

A shiver runs up my spine. I know this is sex, and yet there's always that added danger in the back of my mind. Gio's probably a killer. He knows violence. And it terrifies me, but it also heightens every single interaction we have. The risk level raises the heat level.

"But what if I want you to mark me?" I tease, rolling to my belly and looking over my shoulder at him. "Aren't you going to spank me?"

Gio's smile is feral. "Certainly. And I'm going to fuck that ass tonight. But first, I'm going to remind you who you belong to."

Another shiver.

"How, Gio?" My voice sounds husky, full of lust.

He unzips my skirt and tugs it off, then pulls down my panties. "Put your ass in the air."

I start to crawl up to my hands and knees, but he catches my nape and shoves my head back down. "Just your knees, angel. Keep those tits on the bed."

My pussy gushes arousal.

Gio keeps the hand at my nape, holding me down, even though I'm not going to move and proceeds to spank my ass. As always, the first spanks are the worst. Hot and stingy. Shocking and loud. Then my body adjusts. My ass warms up.

But just as it's starting to feel good, he stops. "Don't move, angel."

When he gets the lube, I think he's going to fuck my

ass now, but then he produces a bulbous stainless steel object. I've never seen one in real life before, but there's no doubt what it is. I blush just at the sight of it.

"Here's what's going to happen, beautiful." He dribbles lubricant over my asshole and then swirls the tip of the buttplug in it. "You're going to wear this while you cook my dinner." He pushes it against my opening, forcing it in an inch, and I mewl at the intrusion. "And I'm going to watch you prance around my kitchen in nothing but your sexy thigh highs, bra and this plug. Deep breath."

I inhale.

"Exhale."

I blow out my breath and he presses the plug forward until it stretches me wide and then, thankfully, seats. The result is a constant pressure on my anus and a full sensation inside.

"Now get up." He gives me a light slap.

I move slowly, almost afraid of jostling the plug. Every movement brings fresh stimulus to my anus. "Oh, boy."

Gio splays his hand on my lower back and pulls me against him. "You okay?"

I love that he checks in, especially after being so dommy.

"Yes," I breathe.

"Then get in my kitchen." He gives my ass another light slap and I scoot forward, shivering at the wealth of sensations coasting through my body. After a few steps, I get accustomed to the plug and sway my ass a bit, knowing he's walking behind, admiring me.

"That's it, gorgeous. Work it for me."

I do. I strut around the kitchen as I prepare two beautiful top sirloin steaks with sautéed mushrooms and an arugula-grape salad with crushed hazelnuts. I'm confident in my meal selection and even more sure of my sex appeal. With Gio, I've become a sexual creature. I don't know— it's like I never really inhabited my body until he came along and woke it up. Now I adore my skin. I'm looking in the mirror, enjoying my reflection, which makes me more inclined to use make up and do something with my hair. Because it's fun, not because I feel like I need to.

I'm falling in love with Gio Tacone.

That is the unfortunate fact.

Unfortunate because I still can't find it in me to fully trust him. After a lifetime of my grandfather grousing about the Tacones, warning me to never, ever get involved with the mafia, it's hard to not fear I'm making a terrible mistake.

But that's my mind.

My heart? My heart's already decided.

He's got the keys.

And my body? Heck, he had this body from day one.

He sits at the breakfast bar now, covering his mouth, his eyes like burning coals. His body is a wound coil, ready to spring. Tension and expectation crackle in the air between us.

I finish preparing the meal efficiently, then shoot Gio a pleading look. "You're not going to make me keep this in during dinner are you?"

I don't know how I can believe Gio's dangerous, because the way his face instantly softens is breathtaking. "Come here, angel." He stretches out an arm.

I sashay out of the kitchen and he loops an arm around my waist and escorts me to the bedroom.

"Ready for your punishment?" he purrs.

"Yes, Mr. Boss."

"Sir. Owner. Master. Boss. Any of those work." He wears a smug grin on his handsome face and my pulse revs with excitement. He takes my hand and pulls it toward the bulge in his pants. "Although right now, I might say you own me as much as I own you, angel."

And that right there is how I knew for sure—

I'm totally, completely, head-over-heels in love with Gio Tacone.

CHAPTER 13

 io

MARISSA and I walk along the shoreline in the morning with steaming lattes. The air is chilly but the sun is strong, glinting off the waves in streaks of silver.

Everything I've done in my life—all the good things, at least—I want to do over with Marissa at my side.

I want to take her to Vegas and show her the Bellissimo. I want to take her to Sicily and show her the Old Country. I want to bring her to all the nicest restaurants. All the beautiful beaches. All the amazing sights this world has to offer.

For now, I'll settle for a walk along Lake Michigan.

I lace my fingers through hers, enjoying the ease between us. The warmth in my body from just having her beneath me. From taking her again against the shower wall afterward.

The image of her prancing around my kitchen with those sexy stockings and bra and my handprints on her ass will forever be at the top of my spank bank album.

But Marissa's getting tense now—nervous. Which means she needs to get home for some reason or other.

I make it easy for her. "What time do I need to get you back, angel?"

"Actually soon. My grandparents are at a wedding and I have to watch Mia, my little cousin."

"I'll watch her with you."

Marissa stiffens and stops walking. "Um, no. You don't have to do that, Gio."

"I want to. I haven't met the child with the thirty-thousand dollar hip yet."

It's supposed to be a joke, but it falls flat, because Marissa takes it as a reminder of what she owes me.

She swallows. "Well, sure. I mean, I guess you could come in for a little while."

"So long as I'm gone by the time your grandparents return?"

She looks relieved at first, until she realizes I'm not happy with her thinking. "Shit, Gio. Please don't ride me on this."

I'm fucking toast when she turns those pleading blue eyes up on me. She's so unbelievably beautiful and enigmatic. One moment she's sweet and subservient, the next, she busts my balls. Sometimes she seems way too young for me. Other times, she's the most mature woman I've ever dated.

I cup her nape and bring her face up to mine for a kiss. "All right," I say after brushing her lips with mine. "I won't ride you." I want to say more, but I like the way her body softens into mine way too much. I don't want her tense again. So I kiss the living hell out of her and walk her back to my place to get the SUV.

Marissa fiddles with the radio on the way. I like how comfortable she's getting with me. There's more ease between us than ever. I just have to be patient with her. Prove I'm worthy.

I can do that.

When we get to her grandparents' place, she gets nervous again. I grab her hand on the way up the sidewalk and it's clammy.

I almost want to tell her she doesn't have to do this. If bringing me home makes her uncomfortable, it's not worth it. But this is a baby step. We need this.

"Lori, Mia, I'm home!" she calls out when we step inside.

Her aunt bustles out. "Oh good, I was just won—" She breaks off when she catches sight of me and freezes in the middle of putting an earring in. "Ah… um…"

"You know Gio, right? From the cafe?"

Her aunt's mouth hangs open. "Um, yeah. Sure. Of course." She shoots Marissa a questioning look as her daughter comes out, limping a little.

"Heyyy, you must be Mia," I say, giving her a broad grin.

She sends me a shy smile. "Hi."

I hold out my hand for a shake. "I'm Gio. I'm a friend of your cousin."

169

"Boyfriend?" Mia asks, stepping forward hesitantly to put her smaller hand in mine.

I give it a little shake and drop it. "Yeah. Boyfriend."

Lori lifts her brows at Marissa with a stunned look.

Marissa shrugs. "Yep." She doesn't quite manage nonchalance.

"Can I have a word with you?" Lori demands, jerking her head toward a bedroom.

Marissa follows her in and I hear their whispered fight. "You're dating a Tacone? Are you freaking nuts? *This* is who you've been spending all that time with? *Him*?"

"So what? It's my business."

"Okay, even if that were true, what were you thinking bringing him here? Are you nuts? I mean, for one thing, Nonno would die of heart failure if he knew. For another—I don't want him around my kid."

I saunter to the doorway and lean my shoulder against it. "I don't eat children," I say mildly. "Contrary to popular belief."

Lori gasps and her face goes pale. Cristo. I hate this feeling. It's not new—I've been the bad guy in the neighborhood since I was a kid. I was raised to be proud of being the bad guy. Only it never felt right on me. Like deep down, I knew I wasn't the bad guy. I was just pretending. Only that's not how it works, is it? I have pulled the trigger before. On guys who deserved it—only on the wicked. I've used my fists to make a point or exact justice more times than can be counted. So yeah. I *am* the bad guy.

It's just that with Marissa... I feel like something else. Like me. Maybe even something good.

"I would never harm anyone in this family. *Lo prometo*. You have my oath." I take a breath, knowing it's too soon, but also wanting it said. I say what I've been planning to say to Marissa's grandparents. "I'm in love with your niece, Lori. Your family is important to me now. And I won't let my family's business ever affect you again."

Lori lets out a little gust of air and swallows. I can tell she doesn't believe me but is maybe too scared to argue.

Marissa's gone pale, too, but I don't think it's from fear. There's wonder mixed in her gaze, along with residual wariness.

"Just give me a chance, huh? Can I ask that much of you? I'll prove to you I'm going to treat Marissa right. I'll never hurt her."

Marissa does that rapid blinking thing she does any time I do something nice for her.

Lori pinches her lips together but picks up her purse with a resigned sigh. She loops it over her shoulder and looks at Marissa, not me. "You are never going to sell this to Nonno. Never." She walks out of the room, shaking her head.

Marissa turns her blue-green eyes on me, which are bright with unshed tears.

I open my arms. "Come here, angel. I'm sorry this is difficult. I really am."

"No, I'm sorry," she sniffs, letting me hold her. But she pulls it together almost immediately and pushes away from me. "Come on, Mia's out there."

We find Mia settled on the couch watching television.

I sit beside her. "What are you watching?"

171

"*The Flash*," she tells me. "It's on Netflix. I've already watched every episode, but I started over."

"Flash, hmm? I haven't heard of him. I guess he's super fast?"

"Yep, super fast. He has to wear that suit or else he'll get hurt by the friction."

"Cool."

Marissa moves around, straightening up, taking out the trash, working in the kitchen.

I lift my chin in the direction of the kitchen. "Is she always working?"

"Always, always," Mia says. "My mom says she's lucky she's still young, but she's going to burn out by the time she's thirty."

I rub my chin. Not on my fucking watch.

The episode ends and Mia hits pause before the next episode begins. "Do you want to play a game?"

"Hell, yes— I mean, heck yes I want to play a game, little lady. What games do you have? Do you play cards?"

"Yes!" She gets up and limps down the hall and returns with a deck of cards. "What do you want to play?"

I pin her with a mock serious look. "Do you play poker?"

She giggles. "No."

"Wanna learn?" I reach in my pocket and pull out my wad of cash. "It involves betting and money. You have a chance to win big, sweetheart."

Yeah, I'm never above a bribe. Especially when it involves a child. Money, sweets or forbidden activities will always win their affection.

I count out five ten-dollar bills and hold them out to

her. Her eyes get wide and she reaches for them, then stops herself mid-air and shoots a guilty glance down the hall.

Shit. Has this child been poisoned against me, too?

"It's all right. You can take it." I continue to hold the money out.

She takes it because—of course—she wants to.

I count myself out another fifty in tens and lay them in front of me. "We don't have poker chips, so we'll just play for the bills here."

"Marissa, angel," I call to the kitchen. "Come and play poker with us."

She rounds the corner with a plate filled with apple slices and peanut butter and raisins. "I don't know how to play poker."

"Mmm." I reach for an apple slice and dip it in the peanut butter. "Are these for me?" I take the plate and make a show of offering it to Mia and then pulling it back when she reaches for it a couple times before I set it down in front of her. "Mia doesn't know how either, so I'll teach you both. I have to get you prepped for when I take you to Vegas."

Marissa shoots me a surprised look but her cheeks color like she's excited by that declaration. Good. She wants to go.

I give Marissa a starting pot of fifty bucks, too and explain the rules of the game, laying out examples of winning hands. "This is a full house. This is two of a kind. This is—"

"Wait, wait, wait. I need a notepad to write these down. I don't think I'll remember."

"I don't need a notepad," Mia declares.

"You think you have it already?" I ask her with a broad smile.

"Yes."

"Good. Let's show Marissa how it goes. For the first few hands we'll play without money and cards face up as practice. Then we'll let the money fly." I waggle my brows and Mia smiles happily at her stack of money.

"If I win, do I get to keep the money?"

"Oh yeah. Definitely. That's what makes it fun."

"Even though it was your money to start with?"

"It's your money now. Yours to lose."

She grabs the money and stuffs it in a pretend pocket. "Forget it, I'm not playing," she says.

I laugh—a big, belly laugh that surprises me. I don't know when I've laughed like that before, but humor on an eight-year-old took me by surprise.

Marissa laughs, too, her eyes soft on me.

I fucking love that look. I want to win it every. Fucking. Time.

We play five or six rounds with cards up until I'm sure they both are getting the hang of it and then I teach them how to bet.

Marissa is conservative with her money, but Mia goes right at it, throwing the bills in and holding her cards up close to her face.

She wins the first hand and gets so excited she jumps up and down and then gasps in pain and hobbles back to the couch.

"You okay, baby?" Marissa runs around to help her, even though she's already sitting. "Did you hurt yourself?"

"I always forget about my bad hip," Mia says to me with a wry smile. "And then I hurt it again."

"Well, I hope you're getting as much mileage out of this situation as you can," I tell her. "You know, making them bring you chocolate cakes and all that."

She giggles.

"My ma had a hip replacement surgery last year and she was the most demanding patient ever. We ran through a whole bunch of nurses before my brother finally hired one who stood up to her and didn't let her push her around."

"Was that Desiree?" Marissa asks.

I shoot her a smile. "It sure was. That's how Junior met her. And then she was a nurse for me when I had an accident," I say to Mia.

"Accident, yes," Marissa says, her gaze dropping to my scar, the flicker of trauma apparent before she hides it.

"Come on, let's play another hand," I say. "Let's see if we can take some money back from the little card shark over here."

Mia cackles with joy as she settles back and pops an apple slice in her mouth.

I win the next hand, then Mia takes two more. When Marissa runs out of money, I fish some more out of my pocket.

It makes her a bit uneasy, taking money from me. People have all kinds of hang ups about money. Some get turned on by it. Some hate it. Most have a love-hate relationship with it. That's Marissa. There's the quickened breath at the sight of a lot of money, but also a furrow of disapproval between her brows. A wariness, like if she

175

takes it, she's eaten the fruit that will land her in Hades for the next seven months.

The next hand I win. I lay my cards down. "I got my lucky hand, ladies. Dead Man's Hand. Two pairs—black aces, black eights. You know why it's called Dead Man's Hand?"

"Why?" Mia demands.

"It originated in the Wild West. It was the hand Wild Bill Hickok had when he was murdered. An unlucky event for Wild Bill, but for some reason, it's always been my lucky hand."

Marissa sucks in a breath. "Well," she says, her tone slightly shaky. "Maybe that's why you were luckier than Wild Bill."

The images of the dream flash through my mind on super-speed. It's not the actual event I see now. Just the new, twisted one. The one where the gun's at Marissa's head.

I lived. I lived. Sometimes it feels like there has to be a *reason* I lived.

And that it's somehow tied up with Marissa.

A chill spins through me. I want it to be a happy reason, like to make Marissa my wife. Run a restaurant with her. But instead it seems like something far darker.

A warning.

I lived to prevent something bad from happening to her.

Marissa

. . .

As if I weren't already falling head over heels in love with Gio, he had to go and be *adorable* with my cousin.

Mia counts her bills, beaming at her new favorite person on Earth. How quickly I was replaced. "I get to keep this, right?" she asks for the eighth time.

Gio winks at her. "You sure do. Buy yourself something nice with it."

I elbow him and he tosses an arm around me.

"Maybe don't tell your mom," I suggest to Mia.

"Why not?" She gives me her full attention now. Kids are so damn smart. She knows something's afoot.

I try to shrug casually. "She might tell you it's too much to accept as a gift and make you give it back." That's not a lie, although it's way more about who the gift came from than how big it is.

"It wasn't a gift, I won it!" Mia retorts.

"Then she'll say she doesn't want you gambling. Just go put it in your treasure box or somewhere safe okay? Or I can keep it for you."

She yanks the bills against her chest. "No way."

And that's when the door opens.

My nonna actually gives a half-shriek, "O-oh-oh!" at seeing Gio.

Gio surges to his feet, ever the gentleman. He greets my grandparents in Italian, as was their custom. "*Buon pomeriggio*, Beatrice, Luigi."

Nonno's upper lip curls slightly as he looks from Gio to me. The betrayal is evident. I brought the enemy into our home. Still, he puts on his act. The one he always puts on for the Tacones when they're in our shop. "Gio, *buon pomeriggio*. How are your brothers?"

Okay, so we're doing chit-chat. Meanwhile, my stomach is a tight twisted ball smashed into my solar plexus.

"Good, good." Gio squeezes my hand and Nonno's eagle eye tracks the movement. "Well, I was just going to be on my way." He turns to Mia. "It was very nice to meet you, young lady." He holds out his hand and she shakes it with an especially vigorous shake to be silly.

I can hardly get my tongue to untangle to speak. I just stay frozen where I am, not even having the manners to walk Gio to the door. Grateful he didn't try to stay longer.

He gives me a small lift of the hand before he shuts the door, and for some reason it breaks my heart. I don't know; there was something stoic and sad about it. Like he was bearing his rejection, but it brought him down.

Dammit.

But I have no time to think about it, because Nonno turns on me immediately. "What was he doing here?"

My instinct is to make something up, to try to minimize this, but there's no story that would fit or work. I just shrug. "He came with me to hang out with Mia."

Nonna's mouth drops open. Nonno's white brows slam down. "What do you mean? Have you been... *seeing* this guy? Is he the one you've been out with?"

My grandparents have to work hard not to interfere in my dating life. They don't want me disappearing like my mom did, so they don't question me too much about where I've been spending my nights. *You're an adult*, Nonna says out loud when I come home. *I'm not going to ask.* As if she really is dying to ask and has to say that out loud to keep herself from asking.

"Yes," I say simply.

More shock and betrayal registers on both their faces, like they were hoping I'd offer some explanation that sat better with them.

"Marissa, after all I've told you about the Tacone men —" My grandfather breaks off when he sees me shoot a pointed look at Mia.

"Mia, time for your bath," my grandmother says, hustling her out of the room. Mia's eyes are wide, and I'm certain she'll be straining her ears from the bathroom.

"Nonno, Gio's not like that. He's not his dad. Or his brother. Brothers. He's a really great guy who plays piano and treats me like a princess."

Nonno rolls his eyes. "For now he does. Just wait until you step out of line or he wants something more than you want to give. Then it will be threats. Violence, even."

I can't breathe. My chest feels too tight. My stomach too rock hard to make room for the expansion of my lungs. "No," I say. "I don't think that's true."

"Is it about the money?" Nonno says and I see the exact moment he realizes what I've done. He staggers back a little, face going pale. "*Mio Dio*. You didn't… No." He shakes his head in disbelief.

It's like the shooting all over again, where time seems to slow. I can see the bad coming, but I'm powerless to stop it. "Mia?" His voice cracks.

All I can do is nod. Admit it.

"No… *no*. How much?"

"It doesn't matter." I try to make my voice come out strong and sure, but it wobbles.

"What was the bargain?" It's barely more than a whisper. "For you?"

"*No!*" My eyes burn. Of course it seems like I whored myself out. Sold myself to the devil. This was the moment I was trying to avoid. This terrible, crushing feeling of shame. Doubt that I mean anything to him at all, other than as a possession. "No, I'm his personal chef. I deliver his meals once a week, that's all. And that's how I found out... I like him."

"You like him? You *like* him? You don't like a Tacone. You watch your back and hedge your bets and make very sure you never cross one. You need to end things with him right away."

I lift my chin. "I'm not doing that, Nonno. He's not what you think. And you'll come to see that."

I grab my things and stomp out to take the L to Michelangelo's, even though I have an hour to spare.

I'm shaking all over, sick to my stomach. Totally unnerved.

I've never rocked the boat with my grandparents. I'm the overachiever. The one who steps in and takes the burdens. The one who never screws up or causes drama.

Right now I'm imploding. My need to be wanted, to be enough, for all to be right in the world is in conflict with my attraction to Gio.

No, it's way more than an attraction. I can't pretend we're about good sex or even the arrangement I made to borrow that money.

Gio and I have something real.

My grandparents are just going to have to accept that.

Gio

THE MINUTE MARISSA gets off work, she comes crashing into my arms.

Thank fuck.

But also… fuck. Because she's upset and exhausted, and I'm not sure I know how to fix this. At least not yet. But I will.

I hold her, kissing her hair and rubbing her back.

"I'm sorry. That was super awkward at my grandparents', and—"

"Shh." I push her away enough to cup her face and lift it. I kiss her downturned mouth. "It's all right for me. How was it for you?"

Her shoulders sag. "Awful. My nonno thinks I'm whoring myself out to you and that you're dangerous."

Anger rips through me, but I draw a deep breath to contain it. "You're not my fucking whore. You're my girlfriend. At least I want you to be. Did you tell him that?"

She blinks rapidly and drops her forehead against my chest. "You always say the right things, Gio."

"*Believe what I say*, Marissa," I stress, because I'm not sure she does. I lost her back there at her grandparents' house. Even though she's here, in my arms, that fissure of doubt I've been working so hard to close just became a giant chasm.

"What can I do for you, angel? I'd do anything."

She sighs and pulls away and that's when I know I'm right. "I just need to go home tonight."

Fuck.

She doesn't mean my home.

And she would have to ask for the one thing I *don't* want to grant her.

Freedom.

"Yeah, okay," I say, dropping my hand into my pocket to pull out my keys. "I'll drive you."

"Thanks." Her shoulders slump as she shrugs on her jacket.

I splay my hand over her lower back and escort her out of the restaurant. "You're tired, angel. Give it a good night's sleep and things will seem better in the morning."

She pokes me with her elbow. "That was the cheesiest line you've ever fed me."

I chuckle. "You're right. That was lame. But also probably true."

She stops and tips her face up to mine. "Thanks for being so understanding." She rises on her tiptoes and hooks a hand behind my neck to kiss me.

Cazzo.

I want her. I always want this girl, and when she kisses me like that, it's hard to turn off the male aggression she produces in me. I walk her backward until her ass hits my car and press my body up against hers. Wedge one thigh between her legs.

"Don't be so fucking sweet," I growl, nipping down her neck. "I don't want to have to take you back inside and fuck you until you can't walk straight."

She giggles, but I still feel the fatigue radiating off her, so I take mercy.

I give her ass a firm, possessive squeeze. "Next time I won't be so lenient," I warn, knowing she likes when I get punitive.

"Mmm," she agrees and kisses me again.

And then it's back on—her lips sliding over mine, her tongue sweeping into my mouth.

I bend my knees and grind my cock at the apex of her thighs until she moans and tugs at my hair.

"For tonight your punishment will be *not* getting fucked," I tell her as I pull away and take in her flushed cheeks, the swollen lips.

She's so fucking beautiful.

"Mean," she murmurs, eyes locked on mine, somehow making the one syllable sound sexy and inviting.

"Yes," I agree, unlocking the car and shifting my weight off her. I open her door and help her in.

I should be content. I'm taking her home, but she's still giving herself to me. These kisses are honest. The intensity of her gaze is real. Everything between us seems normal. Close even.

Why then, do I have this mounting feeling of dread?

CHAPTER 14

$\mathcal{M}$*arissa*

SATURDAY I GO in to help at Milano's. Everyone's there—both my grandparents, Lori, Mia, me. They don't really need me. Maybe I'm just there out of guilt— I don't know. Trying to still be loved despite my disappointing choice in men. Despite my betrayal.

It's our busiest day, and I'm working the front counter. That's why I don't really notice when he comes in.

I take orders and ring people up and then suddenly, *fucking Arnie* is standing across the counter.

Holding a gun.

The room spins. Warps.

I have that freaky fishbowl feeling of nothing in focus but his giant face in front of me. Scratch that, the cold muzzle pointed between my eyeballs.

The cafe goes dead quiet.

The metal at my forehead trembles.

"You lost me my job, you little bitch." He's drunk. "You couldn't give me any of that pussy, but you put out for him, huh? Had to go and spread your legs for the new owner? Did you suck his cock, too? Is that how you got me fired?"

A wild, raucous shaking starts in my knees and travels all the way up my skeleton until every bit of me shudders non-stop. My life is in danger, but what registers more is the humiliation.

He's calling me a whore in front of my grandparents. My eight-year-old cousin.

My aunt.

That's the part I want to stop.

Maybe because my brain can't even contemplate the danger I'm in right now.

And then, it starts to.

The memory of six dead bodies on this floor floods my mind. How much blood there was. What it looks like to see brains splattered on the wall.

Paolo paid for cleaners to come and scrub the place last time.

Who will clean my blood?

Crazy thoughts. I'm having crazy thoughts.

"Huh?" Arnie shouts, spittle flying from his mouth. "Did you blow him real good to get me fired?"

The door opens silently. Somehow I know not to look in that direction. Not to take my eyes from the crazy man in front of me.

The guy who's going to shoot me in front of my family.

And suddenly I want to sob over everything unfinished with Gio. How I haven't really let him in yet. How I want to.

What would it have been like if I had? Would we have found happiness?

Slowly, very slowly, I raise my shaking palms in the air to show my surrender. "I'm sorry, Arnie," I whisper. It's a lie, but I'd say anything right now to keep him from hurting my family. To keep him from open firing in this cafe like Junior did. Gunning down more than just me.

In my periphery, I see the slow approach of a figure. I don't look, but I register dark clothing.

Gio.

In his usual finely tailored Italian suit. Without moving my eyes, I try to track him. He moves ever-so-slowly. Reaches for his waistband in back, but comes up empty.

Because I made him stop carrying a gun.

The cafe is silent. No one else moves. Mia lets out a small whimper behind me.

"I'm sorry, Arnie," I repeat, tears filling my eyes. "Can we talk about this? What would it take to make this right?"

I don't even know how I'm able to form words. My breath is frozen in my throat.

And then in a lightning fast move, Gio grabs the gun from Arnie's hand and smashes him over the head with it. Arnie's knees buckle and he goes down fast, but Gio's already swinging again, smacking his skull with the butt of the gun. Then he drops the gun and uses his fists, smashing Arnie's face over and over again until blood spurts out and the sound of bone cracking bone turns my stomach.

187

"Make him stop," Lori says. The urgency in her tone shakes me out of my shock.

Gio may have ditched the gun, but that doesn't mean he won't kill this guy. In fact, he's already halfway there.

"Make him stop, Marissa," Mia echoes, and it's the terror in her voice more than anything that sends me hurtling around the counter.

I latch on to Gio's arm. "That's enough!"

He's lost it, though. I don't think he even hears me. Gio's in attack mode. Or more likely, kill mode. It's horrifying to see the man you love turn into a deadly weapon. He continues beating Arnie with his other arm, like he doesn't even notice I'm trying to pull him off.

"Gio!" I scream at the top of my lungs.

Now he finally turns and what I see in his expression changes everything.

I see his terror. His eyes are wide and alert. He scans me for injuries as he climbs up, then wraps me up in his arms in a hug so tight I can't breathe.

"Call 9-1-1," Lori tells Nonna.

"I already called," one of the customers says. "Police are on their way."

Gio won't let me go. I need him to set me free. To handle this situation.

"You," Nonno accuses. I don't have to see to know he's talking to Gio. But I'm shocked to hear he's lost his usual amiable, respectful tone when speaking to a Tacone. The venom in his voice is evident this time. "You caused this." His voice shakes with emotion. I've never heard him so upset. "Violence follows you everywhere you go. Why can't you just leave us alone? Leave us out of it? We don't want you here. My granddaughter doesn't want you in her life."

I stiffen and so does Gio.

His embrace eases slowly until it's nothing. I'm standing there alone.

"That right, Marissa?" His voice sounds hollow.

I look around. Arnie's on the floor in a puddle of blood. Mia's sobbing, staring at him. She'll be scarred for life by what she just witnessed.

"Luigi, he just saved your granddaughter," one of the regulars says.

"Yeah," and "That's right," a few others agree.

I want to step back into the circle of those strong arms and let him go on saving me. But my Nonno thinks this is Gio's fault. And Mia's still crying, traumatized by what she saw.

And I'm possibly in shock and unable to make a rational decision.

"Maybe you'd better go," I murmur, not managing to meet his eyes.

The air drops like a bowling ball between us. Heavier than lead. Or maybe that's my heart—I don't know.

"Yeah," Gio says. "Okay. I'm goin'." And just like that, he walks out.

And that's when I realize even practically-speaking I just made a huge mistake. The cops will want to talk to him about what happened.

But that's not why I feel like the walking dead.

It's because when Gio walked out that door, he took my entire heart with him.

~

Gio

I'M JUST FINISHING WASHING the blood off my hands and face when the cops show up at my door. They throw their weight around pretty hard, trying to intimidate me. Trying to make this thing with Arnie into something mafia-related. But I've been a Tacone too long to even answer their questions without a lawyer present, and since they clearly don't have anything to even justify taking me in, they leave.

There's nothing mobster about this situation, even if I was involved.

But that doesn't change how everyone sees it. Luigi was so sure it was my fucking fault.

Maybe it was, I don't know. I didn't mean to beat the shit out of the guy... aw, who am I kidding? I totally meant to beat the shit out of him. He had a fucking gun to Marissa's head. I consider myself extremely merciful for not taking the safety off his gun—yeah, the idiot didn't even know how to use the thing which is why I risked grabbing it from his hand—and shooting him in the head. Or giving him a few more blows with the butt of the pistol and busting his skull open. Or...

No. Planning the guy's death isn't the direction I should be going.

I'm pretty sure I broke some bones in his face and ribs. That will have to do. I'll make sure to visit him in the hospital to let him know if he ever comes near Marissa or her family again, he's a dead man.

Not just that, I'll kill his whole fucking family.

Because you do not threaten what belongs to a Tacone.

And Marissa belongs to me.

At least I thought she did.

But things have changed.

I let her see the violent side of me. The son Don Tacone raised came out today. A brutish, violent man. The kind who has killed with his bare hands.

And what they saw can't be unseen. The little girl—fuck.

That's the part that makes me want to sink myself in Lake Michigan with a set of cement shoes. I fucking adored that little girl—Marissa's cousin. And she saw something she never should have seen.

Beatrice, too. And Lori. And all those customers. The innocent should never have to witness such a thing.

If I'd had my head together, if I hadn't just had the most terrifying sight in my life unfold before my eyes, I would've pulled his ass out of there and beat him to a pulp in the alleyway.

Why the fuck didn't I?

Idiot. Stupid fucking idiot.

I may have just saved my girl only to lose her anyway.

God's got a pretty fucking shitty sense of humor, doesn't he?

I pour myself a glass of scotch and gulp half of it down at once.

And that's when the doorman buzzes. "Luigi Milano here to see you."

I square my shoulders. Good. He's here to bust my balls, I'm sure. But I'm not afraid. I deserve it. And maybe I can finally settle some of the shit between us. Apologize for what my family's done to him. Make things right.

"Send him up."

I take out a tumbler and pour him a glass of scotch, too, not that I think he'll drink it, then let him in the door when I hear the elevator.

He comes in carrying a shoebox under his arm, wearing a tough look of conviction.

"Luigi," I say. "Come in." I escort him to my office. "Have a seat. Scotch?" I push the drink in front of him.

"No." He sits but his face is hard. He sets the old shoebox in front of him.

The power play would be to sit back and wait for him to talk. This is obviously some kind of offensive move. But I push away my usual schtick. Marissa needs me to fix this.

"One million for Milano's. I'll take over the lease, get a team to run the business. You and your family can retire."

Luigi's face goes red. "What? What are you talking about? No! I'm not here to make deals with you, Gio." He shakes his head. "Actually, that's not true. I am here to make one very important deal."

"Does it have to do with what's in the box?" I prompt. I have this nagging sense I should've led with an apology. Explained my position to Luigi—that I'm in love with his granddaughter and want to make things right.

Instead I've gone into my usual wheeling and dealing over scotch, with the air of danger and power around me.

It's exactly what Luigi hates and yet I play the part he expects.

Fuck.

"Wait—" I hold up my hand. "I want to say something first."

But Luigi's already opened the box, and I suddenly know exactly what's going to happen next.

Just like I knew when Marissa showed up here in that skirt and heels.

Fuck.

The box is filled with old cassette tapes—each one is labeled with a date. He also pulls out an ancient cassette recorder. "You know what these are?" he says.

"I have a pretty good idea." As if this day hadn't gone badly enough. My fucking nightmare coming true right there in Milano's. A gun to Marissa's head. My colossal fuck-up that I still haven't figured out how to fix.

And now this.

Blackmail at the hands of my girlfriend's grandfather.

He slides a tape in the cassette player and hits *play*. It's barely audible. There's a ton of noise, but underneath the background sounds and the warped quality, I hear my father's voice, giving orders. *Vinny, you take care of the Hathaway problem. Junior, find out who skimmed from the electronics heist and teach them a lesson. Take Pauly with you.*

Fucking great.

Evidence against my brothers.

"I have dozens of these," the old man says, shaking the box. "I have more at home. More at my lawyer's office."

"You kept them all these years."

He nods. "Insurance."

I'm suddenly bone tired.

Sick of *La Cosa Nostra*. Sick of my family. Sick of being a Tacone.

But mostly sick of this life and living.

"What do you want, old man?" I'm done being kind. It's too fucking hard when no one accepts it from you.

"I want you to stay away from my granddaughter. Get out of that restaurant where she works. Take Milano's as collateral for the money you loaned her, but cut her out of this. You nearly got her killed last year and it's your fault someone pointed a gun at her head again today. And my other granddaughter, who is just a child, had to witness your disgusting violence. Marissa deserves better than this."

I wouldn't be surprised to hear every plant in the apartment just withered with me. I swear I could suck the sun right out of the sky right now with the black hole inside me.

"And in exchange you give me the tapes?"

"No. I keep the tapes, as I have all these years. To make sure you hold up your end of the bargain."

I throw back the rest of my scotch. I've already shut down. We're past the point of me telling Luigi I'm in love with his granddaughter. We're at the point I might kill a man.

No one threatens a Tacone.

That's a motto I was raised with.

But I have no choice here but to fold. Not because I'm afraid of those tapes—although they could be a fucking problem. My dad's already in jail, but if there's evidence on there that would endanger my brothers' freedom, I can't risk it.

But mostly because Marissa loves this old man.

And so, I would never harm a hair on his head.

Would never threaten or strong-arm him.

And he's right. Marissa does deserve better. Everywhere I tried to help her, I only mucked things up. I bought that fucking restaurant to keep Arnie away from her, and it backfired on me. He showed up at her family business and *pointed a gun at her head.*

Cristo. I should've just stuck with what I know. Violence. Threats.

The more I try to be good for Marissa, the more things go wrong.

"Fine," I say dully.

"You'll end things with Marissa?"

"Yeah."

"And stay away from her? Get out of her life forever?"

"Get out, Luigi." I stand and pick up his untouched drink. I throw it back and slam it down on the table. "We're done here." I take the bottle of scotch and walk out of the office, leaving him to find his own way out.

If I had a coffin, I'd crawl in like a fucking vampire right now and never come out.

Instead, I think I land on the bed—I'm not sure. I'm too busy finding my way to the bottom of the scotch bottle.

$\mathcal{M}$*arissa*

BY THE TIME I finish my shift at Michelangelo's, I'm ready to drop dead. My stomach's been in knots since Arnie showed up this afternoon, and I've just been trying to sweep everything from my mind until I have time to unpack it all.

The trouble with that, is my body is a shaky mess. I want to heave, and I was really looking forward to falling into Gio's arms at the end of the night.

But he didn't come.

He's not here.

And that fact alone is what makes the tears start to fall.

He's not outside in the parking lot, insisting he drive me home. There's no message from him on my phone.

I walk to the L station, sniffing, my brain spinning.

Now it's important to me to remember everything. To

look at the puzzle pieces and figure out why Gio's not here.

I told him to leave. Was I horrible about it? Fuck, I can't remember. I just was in so much shock from having the gun pointed at me and then seeing Mia crying like that. Seeing Arnie's blood and the brutal enforcer Gio unleashed.

Gio… My mind skips a few minutes backward in time. The swiftness with which he disarmed Arnie. The power in those fists when he exacted justice.

Gio *saved my life.*

He was a freaking *hero.*

He snatched a gun from Arnie's hand and beat him to a pulp. In most movies that would be a win. He'd get a medal, or at least sighs from every female in the audience.

And I didn't even thank him.

Instead, I kicked him out like he was the bad guy.

How on Earth did Gio become the bad guy for saving my life? My family blamed him for Arnie being there in the first place, but that wasn't his fault. I might have never started something with Gio and the same thing could have happened. Arnie is a dangerous sociopath.

Not Gio.

Dammit.

I pull out my phone. It's too late to call, but I send a text to Gio. *You saved my life and I didn't even thank you. I feel horrible.* It doesn't feel right, it's definitely trying too hard, but I force it with, *Maybe some punishment is in order?*

I hit send, then wish I'd left the last part off. If Gio didn't come tonight, he must have taken offense. He's always at Michelangelo's when I am. Always there to pour me a drink or sweep me into his vehicle. Or fuck me hard over a table.

I wait the whole train ride home, but I get no response.

Huh.

Maybe Gio's asleep. Did he have problems with the police? I know they were going to go get his statement since I fucked up by telling him to leave.

The house is quiet when I get home and I slip into bed, exhausted, but I can't sleep. I keep picking up my phone checking for a return message from Gio.

Hoping I didn't screw up with him one too many times.

~

Gio

I BREAK up with Marissa by text and I want to punch myself in the stomach.

Your grandfather is right. Violence follows me. I don't want to fuck up your bright future. It was fun while it lasted.

Nothing's fun about the fucking text and the reply nearly kills me. *No, Gio. You saved my life, and I want you in it. Forget about my nonno. We can work this out.*

If I weren't already dead, the last living, breathing part of me dies when I text the next message. *We're over, angel. Your debt to me is forgiven. Have a nice life.*

Next, I let Michael know I'm backing out of the deal to buy Michelangelo's.

He's pissed, and I don't give a shit. I hang up on him cussing me out.

And once those two shitty tasks are done, I hit the bottle again and sit down at my piano to play a three-hour rendition of The Rolling Stones' *Paint it Black*.

~

Marissa

WHOEVER SAID time heals all wounds was a douchebag. The pain is getting worse.

The first few days I stumbled through. I somehow managed to show up and do my work, like I always have, although I probably looked like a zombie.

It hadn't really sunk in that Gio broke up with me. That after all that coming on strong, making me believe he just might stick around, he bailed.

But after I found out he pulled out of the purchase agreement for Michelangelo's, it finally hit me that he really wasn't going to come around. He wouldn't be there waiting one day after my shift. He had no plans to play that beautiful baby grand in there.

After that, I couldn't get out of bed. I got a terrible cold and used it as an excuse to stay in my room for the past week. Maybe it's been over a week. I don't even know.

For once in my life, I let everyone else figure out how

to get things done. I don't even come out of my room to eat—they've been bringing food in to me.

I ignore the tap at my door now.

And my aunt ignores my lack of response and comes in anyway.

She sits down on the side of my bed and pulls the covers back from my head. "Jesus. You look like death, Marissa."

"I feel like death," I tell her.

"Maybe a shower or bath would help."

"Mmm." That's me ignoring her suggestion.

"You know, come back to the land of the living?"

"I don't want to." And that's the God's honest truth. I simply can't imagine ever returning to my life again. I'd rather get on a Greyhound to nowhere than pick up where I left off.

"Is this about Gio?" she asks softly. It's the first time anyone around here has spoken his name and I'm unprepared for the emotion that floods to the fore. Tears crowd not just my eyes, but my entire face and throat, making it hot and full.

"I don't want to talk about it," I manage to croak before hiding my face in my pillow again.

"Marissa…"

I ignore her, hoping she'll go away.

"I didn't know he meant this much to you," she finally says.

And then I suddenly *do* want to talk about it. In fact, I sit up and a flood of words come pouring out of my mouth. "Aunt Lori, I didn't want to date him. I mean, Nonno always made the biggest deal about the Tacones and there was the shooting last year. But Gio's the one who got shot. Out on the sidewalk? I saw the whole thing. And I guess he's had nightmares like me. Except in his nightmares I'm the one who's going to get shot." I stop and clap my hand over my mouth. "Oh my God! Do you think it was a premonition? Like fate sent him to make sure I didn't get shot?"

Lori's brow crinkles and she looks at me with sympathy. "No, honey, I don't think—"

"Well, anyway, that's why he felt like he had to protect me and he started coming around. And Lori, he wasn't scary or dangerous. He was kind and generous and protective. He may have hurt the man who pointed a gun at me, but he would never, ever hurt me. I know that in my soul." Tears drip down my face. "I mean, that's why he's gone now. I kept pushing him away, and he decided maybe he is too dangerous for me."

I grab a tissue and blow my nose.

Lori opens her mouth to speak, but before she can, more word-vomit comes from my mouth.

"And the thing is, I didn't want to let him into my life. Because of Nonno and also because… of my mom. You know" —I wave my hand, fresh tears dripping down my face—"how she left? And I was trying to keep him at arm's distance and then"—I blow my nose again—"the minute I let him in, the minute I got used to feeling like maybe I am enough, maybe I won't get abandoned this time…"

I throw myself back on the bed in defeat.

"Oh my God…" Lori whispers, plucking away the

strands of hair glued to my face with tears. "Baby, I'm so sorry. But you've got this all wrong."

"How?" I demand without lifting my head. Without looking at her. I've fixed my unseeing gaze on a point on the wall, and I'm not looking away from it. "Seriously, Aunt Lori. I'm not ever doing this again. Relationships are not worth the pain. There's no point in trusting people to stick around."

A stuttering sound comes out of her mouth. "Well... you pushed him away, right? You told him to leave. And now he's staying away to protect you. So that's not abandonment. That's caring because you *are* enough. You're damn special."

"Whatever." I mutter.

"Marissa... come on. You have to get out of this bed. At least take a shower. Come and sit at the table to eat— Nonna's making manicotti."

"No."

"You have to, Marissa."

"No, I don't."

"Please? Everyone's worried. We just want to see you up and moving around."

"No."

Lori sighs and gets up and leaves. A few minutes later, Mia comes into my room holding the money she won from Gio. "Marissa?" Her voice is small and scared. "I'll give you this if you get out of bed and eat dinner with us."

I push her hand away. "No, baby. That's your money."

She shakes it in front of my face. "I want you to take it. Come and eat with us."

Fuck.

I sigh and throw my legs out of bed. "That was a low blow," I mutter to myself. Everyone knows I'd do anything for Mia.

I take a shower but my aunt was wrong. I don't feel any better for it. In fact, I'd still like to curl up in my bed and die.

"There she is!" Nonna sings when I show up for dinner. She comes over and kisses both my cheeks. "You look better."

"I seriously doubt that," I mutter.

"So, Marissa really cared about Gio Tacone," Lori says.

For fuck's sake. I get out of bed for this? To have my horrible love life discussed at the dinner table? I turn and pin her with a glare.

Fortunately, my grandparents both ignore Lori.

"I love Gio," Mia pipes up, which further destroys me.

"This feels like another abandonment for Marissa. You know, like *Luisa leaving her*? And now she's swearing off relationships forever."

If I weren't in such a state of fuzz-brain, I might pick up on the accusation in Lori's tone. As it is, I barely hear her words, I'm trying so hard to block them out.

"If you're going to talk about me like I'm not here, I'll just go back to bed," I mumble and start to head out.

"No, no, no, no." Lori blocks the doorway. "I'm sorry. I won't say another word. Sit down. Eat some food. It will do you good."

"Food doesn't fix everything," I mutter.

And I'm right. It fixes nothing at all.

〜

Gio

I KNOCK an empty bottle of Jack over when I startle awake to the sound of pounding at my door.

I'm awake, but I'm not fucking getting up. I'm lying on the couch in the same boxer briefs and t-shirt I've been in for days. Maybe weeks. I don't know how long it's been.

I ignore the knocking.

"Gio! Open the fucking door before I break the motherfucker down!"

It's Paolo. Acting like the *stronzo* he is.

"*Vaffanculo*," I call half-heartedly. *Fuck you.*

Growing up, we Tacone brothers made a habit of cursing in Italian so the nuns and non-Italian adults wouldn't know we were saying bad words. Or at least, how bad the words were.

More pounding. If my door wasn't solid wood, it probably would've cracked by now. Is he using his foot? "I said, *open the fucking door.* Now!"

Porco cane. It takes a huge effort to get to my feet, but I do. When I open the door, fucking Paolo punches me in the gut. "That's for missing Sunday brunch and not calling Ma back about it, *stronzo*."

I double over, wheezing. *Cristo*, I'm out of shape after not moving from the sofa for a week. Or maybe it's all the liquor I've been drinking.

The door swings shut behind Paolo as he takes a casual

glance around the place. With bloodshot eyes, I take a look myself. The place is trashed. Empty bottles of liquor everywhere. Takeout boxes.

"Jesus Christ. This place smells like ass. What happened to your cleaning girl?"

"I didn't let her in when she came."

Paolo makes a scoffing sound. "So, what in the hell happened to you?"

"Nothing," I mutter, scratching my belly.

"Bullshit." He peers at me. "Is that about the girl? She dump you or something?"

"Something. Yeah."

"Well, what the fuck happened?"

That's the thing about Italian family. They're always up in your business. Have to know every fucking detail.

"It was Luigi. He showed up here with a box of cassette tapes."

Paolo instantly understands. "No fucking way."

"Yeah. And the one he played implicated both you and Junior. Nothing big, but who knows what else he has. Twenty years of them, he says. Says if anything happens to him, the lawyer will release them."

"Wait, wait, wait. Back up. What did the *testa di cazzo* want?"

I blink my bleary eyes and look around for something else to drink.

Paolo hits my arm with the back of his hand. "To leave the girl alone?"

"Yeah. Exactly."

"Why? You were good to her. Right? You didn't fuck around on her?"

"Of course not." I scrub a hand across my face and pad into the kitchen in my bare feet, looking for something alcoholic.

"Then why?" Paolo demands, trailing me into the kitchen.

I pick up an empty wine bottle and shake it. There's only a swallow left. I tip it up to my mouth. Make that half a swallow.

Paolo grabs the bottle from my hand and gives me an expectant look.

"What? Oh." I turn to look out the window at Lake Michigan. "Do you believe in fate, Paolo?"

My brother gives me a shove. "Shut the fuck up about fate. Just tell me what the hell happened."

Okay. Skip the fate part. The recurring nightmare that warned me my girl was in danger before she was even my girl.

"I beat the shit out of a guy in Milano's."

Paolo whistles. "That's too bad. What happened?"

"See, he had a gun to my girl's head."

Paolo nods like that was definitely enough said. "Surprised you didn't kill him."

I shrug. "I've changed. But not enough, I guess."

"That's bullshit. Seriously, man, that's total bullshit."

I look back out over the water of the lake, the waves as gray as the sky today. "Do you think my life was spared just so I would save hers, Paolo?"

"What?"

"And like, now I've served my purpose?"

Paolo, being the loving, supportive brother he's always been, punches me in the gut again. When I straighten from being doubled over, he slaps my face. "Get in the fucking shower before I beat the shit out of you."

"Nice," I mutter, but I drag my ass to the bathroom. There's no way I'd win a fight against my big brother right now. Even if I had any fight left in me, which I don't. "Real fucking nice."

I stand under the spray of water until it turns cold. Even then, I keep standing under it. I don't wash my hair. I don't soap up. I just stand there and let it drench me.

Hoping it will wash away all the shit I've done and said in my life. Every bad deed. Every act of violence. Everything it means to be a Tacone.

Too bad such a thing isn't possible.

CHAPTER 16

M *arissa*

I'M WORKING until close at Milano's. No customers are in the place, but my nonno's in back, doing inventory. It reminds me of the evening Gio first walked in. Maybe that's why I'm half-expecting him to show up.

Or maybe it's just wild, undying hope.

Like the hope that my mom will one day show up and apologize for missing my childhood.

Yeah, right.

But when I catch the deep tones of Gio's voice coming from the back, my heart surges into my throat.

He's here.

Talking to Nonno. Maybe fixing things.

That's how stupid my mind is.

I go stand just outside the doorway to the storeroom just to be sure my fanciful thoughts are shit. And they are.

It's not Gio, but it sounds a lot like him. "You don't blackmail a Tacone and live to tell about it, old man."

A Tacone. My heart starts racing.

Gio's brother, then. Which one? Not Junior. Must be Paolo.

"You banked on my brother loving that granddaughter of yours too much to kill you, but me? No such qualms, *il vecchio.* I'm fucking ruthless. Especially when it comes to looking after my younger brother."

"If you shoot me, the evidence goes to the police. Twenty years of tapes implicating everyone in your organization."

I shove my knuckles in my mouth to keep from saying anything. My grandfather blackmailed them with old tapes?

Is this the real reason Gio broke up with me?

"Then they go. There is no organization left. The police aren't going to go chasing people down on petty crimes that happened twenty years ago."

"You don't know that." I hear a mixture of fear and defiance in my grandfather's voice.

"You listen to me. We almost lost Gio last year. And when he came back? He was a ghost of his former self. But with Marissa, he came back to life. He was happy— maybe for the first time ever. And you just couldn't fucking take that, could you? What did Gio ever do to you, huh? Your beef is with our old man, but you just can't let it go. You had to get back at him by destroying something beautiful. Tell me, Luigi, does your granddaughter know what you did?"

I draw a deep breath and walk through the door. "Know what?"

Paolo's leaning against a crate, a pistol held casually in his hand, resting on his thigh. My grandfather is squared off to him in the middle of the storeroom.

"*Cazzo*." Paolo immediately stuffs the gun in the back of his pants like he doesn't want me to see it.

"Know what?" I repeat.

Paolo lifts his chin at my grandfather. "Tell her."

My palms sweat. My breath is shaky. "Tell me what, *Nonno*?" I'm already close to tears.

My grandfather's chin juts out. "I told Gio to stay away from you or I'd go to the cops with evidence I've collected over the years."

My lower lip starts to tremble, but it's anger that fills my gut. "Why, Nonno?"

"Why? Because that man is trouble for you. He's violent. You saw what he did to your old boss."

"Gio *protected* me. He saved me from being molested by that boss by buying the restaurant and firing him. And then he saved my life when Arnie showed up here for revenge. Just like he saved our family when Mia needed her surgery. So, if you get that Gio's anything but the hero in this story—in my story—then I don't think you care about me at all." Hot, angry tears course down my face.

Now I understand why Lori used that tone of accusation when she told my grandparents how heartbroken I was. They must all know what Nonno did.

How could they?

The sense of betrayal cleaves me in two.

Nonno spreads his hands. For the first time, he looks uncertain. "Marissa, of course I care about you."

I rip off my apron. "I'm done. I work my ass off to take care of everyone in this family and when I finally find someone who wants to take care of me, this is what you do to him." I throw the apron on the floor. "Well, I won't have it. If you don't destroy every bit of that evidence and make things right with the man I love, you'll never see me again."

It's an insane thing to say. Especially for me—the person so terrified of being abandoned by the people she loves. For me to threaten the end of our relationship is nuts.

But I mean every word of it. I'm not going to let them keep me from the one shot I had at a decent, loving relationship.

"Where are you going?" Nonno calls to my back as I march out the door to the alleyway.

"To see Gio," I mutter.

I'm halfway to the L stop when a gorgeous Porsche 911 pulls up beside me. "I'll drive you, Marissa." It's Paolo.

No more Miss Independent. It's time to accept help when it's offered. Accept and appreciate. I climb in. "Thanks."

"No problem. Listen…" He pauses like he's not sure what to say.

My anger with my grandfather clears enough for me to realize he's in danger.

"He won't turn the evidence in, Paolo," I say quickly. "I'm sure of it. If he really wanted to take anyone down, he would've done it years ago. It was insurance for a moment like this."

"Yeah, I was thinking the same thing. It was a bluff. He's got too much to lose." Paolo shoots me a glance. "I was going to tell you not to worry about him. I would never harm the old man or anyone in your family. Okay?"

"Because Gio cares about me?"

"For sure because of that. But even if he didn't, our families have history. Like you said, your grandfather could've turned those in years ago, but he didn't. And you covered for us when the *bratva* wanted to kill us all. You tried to warn us. I'm not going to throw that away over an old man getting cantankerous."

I let out a little puff of air. "*Cantankerous.* You're a lot more forgiving than I'm feeling right now." I look at his profile. He looks like Gio, only the energy is tougher. Meaner. He's thicker through the shoulders, and the lines on his face make him appear more rugged. "Thank you for trying to fix this, Paolo." I reel, thinking about how different my life might look if I'd never found out the truth. If I went through life thinking Gio threw me away. I never would've trusted in love again. I would've barricaded my heart up even tighter and never let someone in. Instead, right now my heart's been rent in two, emotion gushing out on all sides.

"Marissa… Gio may not be in a fit state to talk when you get there."

Alarm kicks through me. Of course Gio's suffered, too. "What do you mean?"

"I mean, he was pretty broken up over losing you, doll. Just cut him some slack if he's not presentable."

My mind races over how I can contribute to Gio. What would make up for these horrible weeks of being apart.

"Um… can we… do you mind making a stop? I-I'd like to bring some groceries over."

Paolo shoots me a dubious look.

"To make him dinner."

"Ah. Right. I forgot you're a chef. Sure." He changes lanes and gets me to a grocery store. I don't have my wallet with me, or my phone, since I stormed out without taking my purse, but I do have the tip money I made today in my pocket. It should be enough to buy some meat and vegetables. The rest I can improvise.

I just hope I can make things right.

Gio

WHILE I WAS in the shower, Paolo threw out all the bottles and empty food cartons from my place and cracked some windows to air out the place.

The shower helped, but it still didn't bring me back to the land of the living. I've been standing at the window, staring out at the water for God knows how long. Hours, maybe, judging by the way my feet hurt. Or maybe that's just because they're not used to me being upright.

I hear the tap at the door, but I don't move.

It doesn't quite register. Not as something that requires a response.

I turn when the door pushes open, though. Paolo

must've left it unlocked when he left. I blink because I'm pretty sure what I see is a hallucination. Am I sober yet? I can't remember when I finished that last bottle of Jack. This morning? Last night? Is this some kind of drunk dream? Because I see Marissa coming through my doorway, her whiskey-colored hair pulled up in a messy bun on the top of her head, a few pieces falling loose around her pretty face.

She has groceries in her arms, like this is her regular night, and she's here to cook me dinner.

When I don't say anything, she slips into the kitchen.

Oh, my fucking God, this is real. She's actually here.

I scrub a hand over my unshaven face, grateful I'm at least clean. Relatively sober.

Wait… why is she here? I ended things. At least I thought I did. We can't do this. Not without me bringing my entire family down in a shitstorm with the feds.

I make my way to the kitchen and then stop short.

Marissa's stripped off her clothes and is wearing nothing but an apron as she pours olive oil in a frying pan.

I lean in the doorway to watch. That's when I see the tears streaking her face.

"That's pretty, angel," I say softly. She turns and gives me the most vulnerable, adoring look over her shoulder.

It nearly knocks me to my ass.

I walk forward slowly, afraid if I move too fast, I'll pounce. "It would be prettier without the tears, though." I slide my arms around her waist from behind and kiss her neck.

She leans right back into my arms, swaying like she wants to dance.

My brain keeps shouting at me to stop touching her. Get her out of my place.

But I simply can't handle breaking up with her twice. It's too much to bear. I'd rather have this night and die tomorrow than reject one moment of this sweetness.

"Baby," I murmur at the shell of her ear. "I missed you so much."

"I missed you, too," she chokes, fresh tears streaking down her cheeks. The oil starts to smoke in the pan and she turns off the burner. "I heard what Nonno did," she says.

Now I'm dizzy. "*Cazzo*, angel. I'm so fucking sorry."

"No." She turns around, suddenly fierce. "You don't need to be sorry. I'm the one who's sorry. I pushed you away at every turn, and all you wanted to do was give to me. Protect me." The vulnerability flashes on her face again, but she swallows and says, "Love me?"

"*Si, bambina.*" I don't know why it's easier to say in Italian. But I man up and switch back to English. "I love you."

"I want you, Gio."

I don't think she means just sexually. I think she means it in the entirety of having me, which she already has. But my cock reacts strongly to her words, and suddenly her ass is in my hands and I'm lifting her up to straddle my waist as I kiss the ever-loving fuck out of her. Her hips hit the counter and I grind my cock against the flap of apron fabric covering her bare pussy.

"I only want you," I tell her between fierce kisses. Between teeth knocking teeth and tangled tongues. Bruising kisses meant to claim. Punish. Reward.

She gives it back for all she's worth. Her palms grip my face and she moves her lips frantically across mine, twisting and tasting, consuming.

Needing her somewhere I can pound into her without leaving bruises, I carry her out of the kitchen, into my bedroom, where we tear off each other's clothes. Well, I tear off her apron, and she tears off my clothes. I may like to be the guy in charge normally, but her enthusiasm—her desperation—throw me into ecstasy before I even get her pinned to the bed.

And when I do?

Fucking homecoming.

I do a piss-poor job of foreplay, but it doesn't matter. She's wet for me. Which is good, because I'm shoving into her before my brain even registers the command.

I pin her wrists down and surge inside her. She alternates between closing her eyes and getting lost in lust and snapping them open and staring intently into mine. Like she's afraid of losing me.

Like she thinks I'd ever walk away from her again.

"This is it," I tell her, dipping deep, working a circular thrusting motion that I never want to stop. "No more running away from me."

She shakes her head. "No more running," she agrees. "I'm sorry, Gio."

"No. Don't be sorry," I say between thrusts. "I'm not scolding. I'm telling you I'm not letting you go again. This time you stay. Forever."

She does that getting teary thing, so I kiss the fuck out of her again, and then I roll her over and bang her from behind.

It feels so good to be inside her again. So right. I hold her shoulder and disrespect the hell out of her body, and all the while, she makes these desperate moans and uh-ah-uhs that make my dick even harder for her.

And I'm not going to last much longer.

"Are you close, angel? Push up so I can pinch those nipples."

She lifts her chest from the bed, and I tweak and roll one taut nipple between my fingers. "I'm not close," she pants.

Fuck. I try to dial it back.

"I'm *ready*."

And there I go. I'm already spurting before I even go deep. I thrust a few times, then bury myself to the hilt and undulate my hips so I stroke inside her while staying firmly inside.

I watch all the muscles of her back tighten as her cunt squeezes tight. Her ass and thighs go rigid, legs wide, and I'm already sorry it's over because I want to fuck her again.

She's so damn beautiful.

I keep the slow internal stroking until we both stop coming. Even then I don't want to stop. And that's when I realize I forgot a condom.

I'd be a liar if I said I was sorry. I never wanted kids before and I may be forty, but I would give everything to make a family with Marissa. But of course it should've been discussed.

I ease out and drop to my side. "I went in bareback, angel. I'm sorry, I lost my head. I promise I'm clean."

"I know," she murmurs, turning her face toward me.

I stroke down her spine, admiring the gentle curve. I settle my palm on her ass and cup it. "It doesn't matter because I'm keeping you," I declare, although I watch her face closely as I go in for a kiss.

She's happy. I don't know how I can tell, but I can. She never wanted me to give her up, despite all her pushing away.

"I'm sorry I didn't fight to keep you, angel. I just couldn't go up against someone you love. Someone who cares about you and wants the best for you."

Her jaw sets and she shakes her head. "If he cared about me he wouldn't have hurt me this way."

I tug the scrunchie holding her mussed hair in the loose bun on top of her head and watch the honey-colored locks tumble down to her shoulders. "How did you find out?"

"Paolo came over to have a discussion with him."

A jolt of alarm runs through me. I sit up. "Oh shit."

"No, no, no." She grabs my arm, also sitting up. My brain stutters at the sight of her small breasts, but I jerk my attention back to the problem at hand. Namely—my brother. "It's all right. He told me he would never hurt him." Tears fill her eyes. "He actually gave my grandfather quite a speech about how…" She swallows.

Still alarmed, my brows dip down. "How what?"

"How happy you've been with me?"

I grab the back of her head and smash my lips over hers again. "So fucking happy," I tell her. "And I'm done with you not being happy, Marissa. I'm buying Milano's so your grandparents can retire. And you and I are opening our own restaurant, with you as head chef. And a piano. And a manager who does all the shit we don't want to do."

When she tears up, I push her back down on the bed and cover her slender body with mine. "It's settled, Marissa. You're mine. Say it, now."

She blinks her watery eyes. "I'm yours, Gio," she whispers.

"Say it louder."

"I'm yours."

I shake my head and say firmly, "I'm not letting you go."

She reaches for my face and pulls me down. "You'd better not."

I slide my lips over hers, exploring her softness, tasting her sweetness. "I love you, angel."

She loops both arms around my neck. "I love you, too, Gio."

And then I'm suddenly famished, since I haven't eaten in... I don't know—days. "Were you making something in the kitchen, beautiful?"

The smile that stretches across her face makes my heart double-pump. "Yes, I was. Hungry?"

"Starving, angel."

"Good." She slides out of bed, like serving me is her favorite thing. "I'll make us some dinner."

I want to sigh like a girl.

Now I'm certain of the reason my life was spared. It was to make sure Marissa's life was spared, too. Because we were destined for each other. To give and receive and make each other happy. And be happy together, because I know the Dr. Phil shit about it not being all on the other person making you happy.

I trail after my beautiful chef, watching the twitch of

her bare ass as she walks, tying the apron on around her waist.

Even if I died tomorrow, I'd die happy. Fulfilled. So different from how I felt about my life last year when that bullet went through my flesh.

All I needed was a reason to live.

And now I found her.

EPILOGUE

 *aolo*

"THE FOOD WAS EXQUISITE," Ma gushes as the waitstaff clear our plates. It's the soft opening of Giovanni's, Marissa and Gio's new downtown restaurant. Gio bought a commercial property right on the lake near their apartment, with wall-to-wall windows looking out over the water. People will come here for the views alone, never mind Marissa's food. Although based on the family gathering she hosted last week and what I tasted tonight, she's going to knock that part out of the park, too.

And the piano? I don't know why it makes me laugh my ass off. Maybe just because I remember Gio dreaming of his piano bar when he was like six years old.

And now he's doing it.

Why the fuck not?

The guy came back from the dead. That would make me want to pursue all my lost opportunities, too.

The whole family's here—at least all of the Chicago branch plus Nico, who managed to sneak away from his obligations running the Bellissimo, and Marissa's family too.

I shook Luigi's hand when he came in. I'm not gonna hold a grudge. We had a couple conversations that involved me throwing my weight around a bit. Now everything's resolved.

He gave me the tapes. Gio bought out Milano's and forced their retirement. He and Marissa re-opened it as a wildly popular lunch-spot, rejuvenating the entire block.

Marissa's queen of the place tonight, wearing a slinky teal dress and playing hostess. Her kitchen staff, including a girlfriend from the restaurant where she used to work, prepared her creations tonight.

Gio's been at her back, showing his claim, protecting his prize.

Again, why the fuck not? He deserves her.

Now that dessert is being served, Gio finds his way to the piano, same as ever. He sits down and plays a song that's familiar. A Train song, I think—that cheesy *Marry Me*. When the next song he plays is Bruno Mars' *Marry You*, I start smiling. He's not singing the lyrics, so I don't know if anyone's caught on yet.

More importantly, I don't think Marissa's caught on yet.

I wait for the next song. This time Gio turns on the mic and sings—something he doesn't often do, even though he has a great voice. It's Dean Martin's *Marry Me*.

Ma gasps and that makes everyone sit up and listen.

"Hey, Marissa," I call out. "I think your man has something to ask you."

Marissa surges to her feet, then promptly sits back down again, then stands, covering her mouth and blushing.

"Go on, get up there," her aunt urges, nudging her to the piano.

Gio finishes the song in total Gio style—lady-killer that he used to be. When he's done, he grabs Marissa around the waist and pulls her down onto his lap in front of everybody. The older people titter nervously while the rest of us cheer.

"Marissa, I love you. I think you know by now I'm never letting you go." More nervous laughter from the family. "Let's make it official, angel. Will you wear my ring?" He produces a ring box from his jacket pocket and pops it open. There's a pear-shaped diamond in there the size of a fucking dime.

Marissa tears up while she laughs. "Yes, Gio. I'm not letting you go, either." She takes the ring and slides it on her finger.

My phone buzzes, and seeing it's a call from Stefano, I stand and walk out to the coatroom to take it. "Gio just proposed to his girl," I tell our youngest brother.

"Yeah? Tell him congratulations for me. Bachelor party at the Bellissimo of course."

"Naturally, naturally. What's up?"

"Listen, we have a problem and I wondered if you could take care of it."

"Yeah? What is it?"

"I just found out some hacker's been micro-skimming

every transaction from the casino accounts for the past six years. About a hundred fifty grand total. We traced the money to an off-shore account. Only money in it is from The Bellissimo. Only money out? Tuition payments to Northwestern University."

"Now I see where I come in. So, some guy's using it to put his kid through college?"

"Actually, I think the kid is the hacker. Emancipated at age sixteen, she's now a graduate student in computer science. Name is Caitlin West. I'm sending over a picture and address right now."

He sends the photo and just like that, my dick gets hard. She's definitely fuckable. A red-hot dark-haired geek in giant black-framed glasses and candy-colored lip gloss stares back at me with a saucy look. She looks like the kind who wears a messy bun and threadbare t-shirts to the library, but on weekends secretly sneaks out in a tight leather corset and bootie shorts to whip men at the local dungeon.

"Well, well, well, my hot little hacker," I murmur, staring at the screen. "It's time to pay the piper."

THANK you for reading Dead Man's Hand. For a bonus epilogue of their engagement night, be sure to sign up for my newsletter at http://owned.gr8.com. If you're already a subscriber, the links to bonus material is at the bottom of every newsletter.

WANT MORE? READ AN EXCERPT
FROM WILD CARD

ild Card (Vegas Underground, Book 8)
Caitlin

FISTS AT BOOB LEVEL, elbows back, I lead my dance cardio class through some booty shaking to the song, *Sweet but Psycho*.

Yeah, it's pretty much my theme song.

"Step touch, throw your hand down in front," I sing into the headset, exaggerating the movements to help the class follow along.

Dance cardio is my jam. I teach it four nights a week at the campus rec center and take other movement classes on the off-nights. Anything to keep me moving, which probably seems strange for a computer science geek.

It does border on obsessive, but it's not one of those body-hatred kind of things. I'm not working out to achieve some body ideal or to look a certain way.

I just need to move. I have a hard time staying in my body, otherwise.

Dissociative disorder is the official diagnosis. I check out when things get intense for me. Movement helps. Pain and sex work even better.

General consensus—I'm broken.

But that doesn't matter much, because my time is running out.

The siphon I put on the Tacone family's casino business—the one where I skimmed a fifth of a penny from every transaction—got shut down two weeks ago.

And even though I used an off-shore account for storing the funds before they paid for my brother's and my college tuition, there's a decent chance I'm going to end up swimming with the fishes, as they say.

But I knew that going into my little revenge scheme.

"Wide second position, deep breath in." I start the cool down. It's always over too soon. I lead the class through the closing stretches and thank them all for coming.

"Thank you, Caitlin." My students wave and smile as they leave. Here, I'm almost normal. I could be just like any of them. A pretty, wide-smiling graduate student getting her workout.

It's when people get to know me a little better they see my crazy. Decide I'm the girl to give a wide berth around. Which is totally fine with me.

I grab my towel and head to the showers, picking up my phone to check messages. Not that I ever have any. It's just an anxious habit from when my brother Trevor was still in foster care, and I would freak out if he didn't contact me every day to let me know he was still alive.

Still okay. Not living the nightmare I'd lived.

It's one of the many quirks I have the Tacones to thank for. The side effect of having a dad murdered by the mob.

Except now that I've had my revenge, now that they're coming for me, I'm thinking I shouldn't have stirred the hornet's nest.

I was probably better use to Trevor alive than dead. Even if I did generate enough funds to pay our college tuition.

I'd better warn him. I dial his number and he picks right up.

"Hey, Caitie." He's the only person I let call me that.

"Hey, Trevor. Everything okay?"

"Yeah. Why wouldn't it be?" It's sometimes weird to me how normal he turned out compared to me. But he had a decent foster family. And he had me.

I had only ugliness and myself to rely on.

"Hey, I have to tell you something, but it's going to be fine," I say quickly, just to get the words out. I've tried to tell him four other times since the money got cut off, but chickened out every time.

"What is it?"

"Um, I may have hacked a company I shouldn't have messed with."

"Oh shit. What happened? Are you in jail?"

"Nope, not jail. It probably won't go that route. Do you remember who killed Dad?"

Trevor goes dead quiet. When he speaks, his voice sounds scared. "Tell me you didn't."

"I did. Anyway, they probably won't figure it out, but

if they do, you remember the place we used to say we'd meet up if anything bad happened with foster care?"

I don't know why I'm speaking in code. It's not like the mafia are in the locker room right now. Or bugging my phone.

"I remember."

"If I have to run, that's where I'll go. Okay?"

"Shit, Caitie. This is bad. Are you crazy?"

"That's what they say," I remind him in a sing-song voice. "Anyway, nothing's going to happen. I thought I should tell you just in case."

"Maybe you should go hide there now."

"No, I don't even know if they'll trace it to me. But if they do, I'll figure it out. I don't want you to worry."

"Yeah, I'm definitely worried."

My chest warms. Trevor's the only good in my life.

"Well, don't. You know me—I can take care of myself. I'll figure it out. Just be cautious about any texts from me and don't give up my location if anyone comes asking."

"I won't. Shit, Caitlin."

"It's okay. I promise. I'll text you tomorrow."

"All right. Be careful."

"I will." I hang up and shove my phone down in my bag before I strip out of my sweaty clothes and step in the shower.

If only I believed I have this all under control.

I rinse off with the *Sweet but Psycho* song on repeat in my head.

~

Paolo

I BREAK into the apartment of Caitlin—aka *WYLDE*—West using the key I had made by a locksmith who owed me a favor. I sent one of my henchmen over to watch her for the past week and give me the deets on her habits, so I know she's teaching her dance cardio class now.

I know she'll be home soon, and I'm looking forward to putting the surprise on her when she arrives.

Intimidation is an art form I've spent a lifetime perfecting, and I'm going to scare the piss out of the little hacker who targeted my family's casino coffers.

As the second son of now imprisoned Don Tacone, head of the biggest Chicago crime family, I learned how to crack my knuckles and posture practically as a toddler. How to give a beatdown by age six.

Most of the time, my reputation and the flash of a gun do all the work necessary. It's rare I have to actually hurt anyone or make a plain threat.

So when my brother asked me to take care of our hacker, I was happy to do it. Especially after I saw a picture of the computer geek. The moniker Wylde seems to fit her. It's not the mess of long thick hair or black glasses. It's the pink lip gloss on her smirking mouth that makes me think she's not the antisocial nerd you might expect of someone with her exceptional skills.

The place is tiny—a studio, I guess they call it—with the kitchen on one wall and the bed on the other and a tiny bathroom off the living / dining section. It's a mess. Clothes everywhere. Dirty dishes on every surface.

I pick up a miniscule white thong with one finger.

Nerds in hot panties. That could be a whole fetish. Kinda goes with the sexy librarian thing. I toss the panties in her hamper and continue my perusal.

Stacks of books and computer equipment line the walls and desk. An old bike is parked against one wall, helmet hanging from the handlebar.

I wander around, looking through her things. Ramen and baked beans in the cupboards. Frozen burritos in the freezer. At least she's not living large on our cash.

According to my brother, Stefano, all the stolen money was transferred from an off-shore account straight to the bursar's office of Northwestern University. But if I'm supposed to think it's noble that she only steals for her education, I don't. She fucked with the wrong family.

I stop to examine her bulletin board. Schedules from local yoga and dance studios are pinned over restaurant takeout cards. There's only one photo—of Caitlin and a young man. I pull it down and examine it.

It's the younger brother, Trevor—I see a family resemblance.

He's my ace in the hole. I have a guy watching the twenty-year-old kid who is an art student at the same university. No way my little hacker is going to try any funny business when I hold her brother's balls in a vise.

She'll return our money—steal it from someone else or do whatever she needs to do—and I'll consider letting both of them live.

Normally that wouldn't be Tacone policy, but she's a chick.

And a hot one at that.

Plus, I don't hurt women.

I look through her closet, smiling when I find the clothes I half expected or hoped to find. The vibe I got was right. She has kinky shit—Fishnets. Bootie shorts. Ripped sheer tops. Stripper gear, only she's not a stripper.

I fucking *knew* this girl was freaky.

I swear I could tell it from the photo. The computer geek thing just doesn't sit on her, despite the big black glasses and sloppy clothes. Something about her just screams sex. Maybe it's the candy-colored lip gloss on that wide-mouthed pout. Or the way she holds herself. She just *fucking embodies* carnal pleasure.

And that's why I've been looking forward to this meeting all week.

I glance at the clock. Almost showtime. I throw the clothes tossed over the easy chair onto the floor and make myself at home to wait.

I don't even bother taking out a gun to rest on my thigh like I might with a dude.

She'll be scared enough to find me in her apartment.

And I shouldn't let that give me a hard-on, but it does.

But even with my research and my own conjectures, I'm still unprepared for the hot sexy mess of a hacker who blows in.

She enters her apartment with earbuds in her ears, apparently still jamming out to her workout playlist. She's in a pair of yoga pants and puffy jacket, which she instantly strips to dump on the floor. Underneath, she's wearing a crop top that shows off a perfectly toned midriff below a pair of perky tits. Her dark hair is piled on top of her head in a thick, messy bun and she's wearing that bright lip gloss that makes me think about how that mouth would look around my dick.

She doesn't notice me as she comes in. She doesn't notice much of anything. She appears to be lost in thought as she walks straight to the kitchen, pours herself a bowl of Golden Grahams cereal and milk and starts eating standing up.

Only then does she turn and spot me.

The cereal bowl clatters to the floor as her scream pierces the air. Milk splatters fly everywhere.

Her wide eyes lock on mine, that pretty mouth opens.

But she recovers way faster than I expect. Just one short scream and she goes silent.

"Hello, Caitlin."

"Oh." Her palm travels down her toned belly, wiping at the milk splatters, then she dries it on her ass. And a very fine ass it is.

"The Tacones sent you?" She sounds breathless. Good. She was expecting me.

"I sent myself."

"Mr. Tacone, then."

And that's when I realize my usual intimidation schtick is a total and complete fail.

Because little miss hacker slowly slides her hand between her legs, holding my gaze while she curls her fingers there, touching herself like she's watching porn.

Or rather, like she's the porn star and she knows she owns me with that simple move.

READ NOW

WANT FREE RENEE ROSE BOOKS?

Click here to sign up for Renee Rose's newsletter and receive a free copy of *Theirs to Protect, Owned by the Marine, Theirs to Punish, The Alpha's Punishment, Disobedience at the Dressmaker's* and *Her Billionaire Boss*. In addition to the free stories, you will also get special pricing, exclusive previews and news of new releases.

ABOUT RENEE ROSE

USA TODAY BESTSELLING AUTHOR RENEE ROSE loves a dominant, dirty-talking alpha hero! She's sold over a half million copies of steamy romance with varying levels of kink. Her books have been featured in USA Today's *Happily Ever After* and *Popsugar*. Named Eroticon USA's Next Top Erotic Author in 2013, she has also won *Spunky and Sassy's* Favorite Sci-Fi and Anthology author, *The Romance Reviews* Best Historical Romance, and *Spanking Romance Reviews'* Best Sci-fi, Paranormal, Historical, Erotic, Ageplay and favorite couple and author. She's hit the *USA Today* list five times with various anthologies.

Please follow her on:
   Bookbub | Goodreads | Instagram

Renee loves to connect with readers!
www.reneeroseromance.com
reneeroseauthor@gmail.com

OTHER TITLES BY RENEE ROSE

Vegas Underground Mafia Romance

King of Diamonds

Mafia Daddy

Jack of Spades

Ace of Hearts

Joker's Wild

His Queen of Clubs

Dead Man's Hand (coming soon)

More Mafia Romance

The Russian

The Don's Daughter

Mob Mistress

The Bossman

Contemporary

Black Light: Celebrity Roulette

Fire Daddy

Black Light: Roulette Redux

Her Royal Master

The Russian

Black Light: Valentine Roulette

Mastered by the Zandians

Zandian Lights

Kept by the Zandian

The Hand of Vengeance

Her Alien Masters

Regency

The Darlington Incident

Humbled

The Reddington Scandal

The Westerfield Affair

Pleasing the Colonel

Western

His Little Lapis

The Devil of Whiskey Row

The Outlaw's Bride

Medieval

Mercenary

Medieval Discipline

Lords and Ladies

The Knight's Prisoner

Betrothed

Held for Ransom

The Knight's Seduction

The Conquered Brides (5 book box set)

Renaissance

Renaissance Discipline

Ageplay

Stepbrother's Rules

Her Hollywood Daddy

His Little Lapis

Black Light: Valentine's Roulette (Broken)

BDSM under the name Darling Adams

al Play

Yes, Doctor

Master/Slave

Punishing Portia

Made in the USA
Coppell, TX
14 March 2021